"How did you find me?" Willow whispered.

"A private detection agency. They've been trying to trace you for months," Jai imparted, his wide, sensual mouth compressing at that unfortunate fact. "I only wish I'd found you sooner."

"I can't imagine why you've been trying to find me," she confided.

"But isn't it fortunate that I did?" Jai said smoothly as he stroked a gentle finger through the spill of Hari's black hair. "You must realize that you cannot stay in such a place with my son."

Paper pale at that quiet declaration, Willow gazed back at him. "*Your*...son?" she almost whispered, shaken by the certainty with which he made that claim.

"He is my image. Who else's son could he be?"

Lynne Graham was born in Northern Ireland and has been a keen romance reader since her teens. She is very happily married to an understanding husband who has learned to cook since she started to write! Her five children keep her on her toes. She has a very large dog who knocks everything over, a very small terrier who barks a lot and two cats. When time allows, Lynne is a keen gardener.

Books by Lynne Graham

Harlequin Presents

The Greek's Blackmailed Mistress
The Italian's Inherited Mistress

Conveniently Wed!

The Greek's Surprise Christmas Bride

One Night With Consequences

His Cinderella's One-Night Heir

Billionaires at the Altar

The Greek Claims His Shock Heir
The Italian Demands His Heirs
The Sheikh Crowns His Virgin

Vows for Billionaires

The Secret Valtinos Baby
Castiglione's Pregnant Princess
Da Rocha's Convenient Heir

Visit the Author Profile page
at Harlequin.com for more titles.

Lynne Graham

INDIAN PRINCE'S HIDDEN SON

Recycling programs
for this product may
not exist in your area.

ISBN-13: 978-1-335-14825-4

Indian Prince's Hidden Son

Copyright © 2020 by Lynne Graham

This edition published by arrangement with Harlequin Books S.A.

For questions and comments about the quality of this book,
please contact us at CustomerService@Harlequin.com.

Harlequin Enterprises ULC
22 Adelaide St. West, 40th Floor
Toronto, Ontario M5H 4E3, Canada
www.Harlequin.com

Printed in U.S.A.

INDIAN PRINCE'S
HIDDEN SON

CHAPTER ONE

IT WAS A dull winter day with laden grey clouds overhead. Fine for a funeral as long as the rain held off, Jai conceded grimly.

In his opinion, English rain differed from Indian rain. The monsoon season in Chandrapur brought relief from the often unbearable heat of summer, washing away the dust and the grime and regenerating the soil so that flowers sprang up everywhere. It was a cool, uplifting time of renewal and rebirth.

His bodyguards fanned out to check the immediate area before he was signalled forward to board his limousine. That further loss of time, slight though it was, irritated him because, much as he knew he needed to take security precautions, he was also uneasily aware that he would be a late arrival at the funeral. Unfortunately, it was only that morning that he had flown in from New York to find the message from Brian Allerton's daughter awaiting him, none of his staff having appreciated that that message should have been treated as urgent.

Brian Allerton had been a Classics teacher and house master at the exclusive English boarding school that Jai had attended as a boy. For over two hundred years, Jai's Rajput ancestors had been sending their children to England to be educated, but Jai had been horribly homesick from the moment he'd arrived in London. Brian Allerton had been kind and supportive, encouraging the young prince to play sport and focus on his studies. A friendship had been born that had crossed both age barriers and distance and had lasted even after Jai went to university and moved on to become an international businessman.

Brian's witty letters had entertained Jai's father, Rehan as well. A shadow crossed Jai's lean, darkly handsome face, his ice-blue eyes, so extraordinarily noticeable against his olive skin, darkening. Because his own father had died the year before and Jai's life had changed radically as a result, with any hope of escaping the sheer weight of his royal heritage gone.

On his father's death he had become the Maharaja of Chandrapur, and being a hugely successful technology billionaire had had to take a back seat while he took control of one of the biggest charitable foundations in the world to continue his father's sterling work in the same field. Jai often thought that time needed to stretch for his benefit because, even working night and day, he struggled to keep up with all his responsibilities. Suppressing that futile thought, he checked his watch and gritted his teeth because the traffic was heavy and moving slowly.

Brian's only child, Willow, would be hit very hard by the older man's passing, Jai reflected ruefully, for, like Jai, Willow had grown up in a single-parent family, her mother having died when she was young. Jai's mother, however, had walked out on Jai's father when Jai was a baby, angrily, bitterly convinced that her cross-cultural marriage and mixed-race son were adversely affecting her social standing. Jai had only seen her once after that and only for long enough to register that he was pretty much an embarrassing little secret in his mother's life, and not one she wanted to acknowledge in public after remarrying and having another family.

It was ironic that Jai had come perilously close to repeating his father's mistake. At twenty-one he had become engaged to an English socialite. He had been hopelessly in love with Cecilia and had lived to regret his susceptibility when she'd ditched him almost at the altar. In the eight years since then, Jai had toughened up. He was no longer naive or romantic. He didn't do love any more. He didn't do serious relationships. There were countless beautiful women willing to share his bed without any promise of a tomorrow and no woman ever left his bed unsatisfied. Casual, free and essentially *forgettable*, he had learned, met his needs best.

As the limousine drew up outside the cemetery, Jai idly wondered what Willow looked like now. Sadly, it was three years since he had last seen her father, who had turned into a recluse after his terminal illness was diagnosed. She had been away from home studying on his last visit, he recalled with an effort. He had not regretted her absence because as a teenager she had had a huge crush on him and the amount of attention she had given him had made him uncomfortable back then. She had been a tiny little thing though, with that hair of a shade that was neither blond nor red, and the languid green eyes of a cat, startling against her pale skin.

Willow stood at the graveside beside her friend, Shelley, listening to the vicar's booming voice as he addressed the tiny group of mourners at her father's graveside. Brian Allerton had had no relatives and, by the time of his passing, even fewer friends because as his illness had progressed he had refused all social invitations. Only a couple of old drinking mates, one of whom was a neighbour, had continued to call in to ply him with his favourite whiskey and talk endlessly about football.

A slight stir on the road beyond the low cemetery wall momentarily captured Willow's attention and her breath locked in her throat when she realised that a limousine had drawn up. Several men talking into headsets entered the graveyard first, bodyguards spreading out in a classic formation to scan their surroundings before Jai's tall, powerful figure, sheathed in a dark suit, appeared. Her heart clenched hard because she hadn't been expecting him, having assumed that the message she had left at his London home would arrive too late to be of any use.

'Who on earth is *that*?' Shelley stage-whispered in her ear, earning a glance of reproof from the vicar.

But no, contrary to Willow's expectations, Jai, technology billionaire and media darling, had contrived to attend and, even though he had missed the church service, she was impressed, hopelessly impressed, that he had actually made the effort. After all, her father had, during his illness, stopped responding to Jai's letters and had turned down his invitations, proudly spurning every approach.

'Wow…he's absolutely spectacular.' Shelley sighed, impervious to hints.

'Talk about him later,' Willow muttered out of the corner of her mouth, keen to silence her friend.

Shelley was wonderfully kind and generous but she wasn't discreet and she always said exactly what she was thinking.

'He's really hot,' Shelley gushed in her ear. 'And he's so tall and *built*, isn't he?'

Jai had been hugely popular at school when Willow was growing up in the little courtyard house that had gone with her father's live-in employment. The last in a long distinguished line of Rajput rulers and warriors, Prince Jai Singh had been an outstanding sportsman and an equally brilliant scholar and Willow had often suspected that Jai had been the son her father would've loved to have had in place of the daughter who had, sadly, failed to live up to his exacting academic standards.

And even though it had been three years since Willow had seen Jai she still only allowed herself a fleeting glance in his direction and swiftly suppressed the shiver of awareness that gripped her with mortifying immediacy. After all, a single glance was all it took to confirm that nothing essential had changed. Jai, the son of an Indian Maharaja and an English duke's daughter, was drop-dead gorgeous from the crown of his luxuriant blue-black hair to the toes of his very probably hand-stitched shoes. Even at a distance she had caught the glimmer of his extraordinarily light eyes against his golden skin. His

eyes were the palest wolf-blue in that lean, darkly
handsome face of his, a perfect complement to his
superb bone structure, classic nose and perfectly
sculpted mouth.

Jai, her first crush, her only infatuation, she conceded in exasperation, her flawless skin heating
with the never-to-be-forgotten intense embarrassment of her teenaged years as the mourners came,
one by one, to greet her and she invited them back
to the house for an alcoholic drink as specified by
her late parent, who had ruled against her provid-
ing traditional tea and sandwiches for the occasion.
Even so, she would have to make exceptions for the
vicar and for Jai.

As Jai strode towards the small group, his keen gaze
widened infinitesimally, and his steps faltered as
soon as he recognised Willow, a tiny fragile figure dressed in black, with an eye-catching water-
fall of strawberry-blond waves tumbling round her
shoulders that highlighted bright green eyes and a
lush pink mouth set in a heart-shaped face. The shy,
skinny and awkward teenager, he registered in surprise, had turned into a ravishing beauty. His teeth
clenched as he moved forward, inwardly censuring
that last observation as inappropriate in the circumstances.

A lean hand closed over hers. 'I apologise for my late arrival. My deepest condolences for your loss,' Jai murmured softly.

'Hi... I'm Shelley,' her friend interrupted with a huge smile.

'Jai...this is my friend, Shelley,' Willow introduced hastily.

Jai grasped Shelley's hand and murmured something polite.

'Come back to the house with us,' Willow urged him stiffly. 'My father would've liked that.'

'I don't wish to intrude,' Jai told her.

'Dad wouldn't see anyone while he was ill... It wasn't personal,' Willow told him chokily. 'He was a very private man.'

'Your dad was right eccentric,' Shelley chimed in.

'His desire for privacy must've made his illness harder for you to deal with,' Jai remarked shrewdly. 'No support. I know you have no family.'

'But Willow does have friends,' Shelley cut in warmly. 'Like me.'

'And I am sure she is very grateful for your support at such a difficult time,' Jai responded smoothly.

That reminder of her isolation hit Willow hard. Losing her father, who had been her only parent since her mother had died when she was six, was already proving even tougher than she had envisaged. Worse still, the reality that they were stony broke, for those last months had broken her father's heart and hastened his end. Evidently fantasising about leaving his daughter much better off than they had been, her father had, as his life had drawn to a close, begun using his pension fund to play with stocks and shares without seeming to grasp the risk that he was taking.

Convinced that he was onto a winning strategy, Brian Allerton had been devastated when he'd lost all his savings. He had spent his last months grieving for the mistake he had made and the truth that he was leaving his daughter virtually penniless. They were fortunate indeed that her father had arranged and settled the expenses of his own funeral as soon as he had appreciated that his condition was incurable. But only their landlord's forbearance had kept a roof over their heads as they had inevitably fallen behind with the rent, and that was a debt that Willow was determined to somehow settle.

'I'll get by,' she parried with a stiff little smile. 'Dad and I were always alone.'

'Let me give you a lift,' Jai urged smoothly.

'No, thank you. Our neighbour, Charlie, is waiting outside for us,' she responded with a rueful smile that threatened to turn into a grimace.

Shelley, proclaiming that *she* would've enjoyed the opportunity to travel in a limousine, hurried after

Willow in dismay as she turned on her heel to head out to the ancient car awaiting them beyond the cemetery wall. Willow, not having noticed her friend's disappointment, was all of a silly flutter, and furious with herself, butterflies darting and dancing in her tummy and leaving her breathless as a schoolgirl simply because she had been talking to Jai. Any normal woman would have grown out of such immature behaviour by now, she told herself in mortification. Unfortunately, through living with and caring for her father and lack of opportunity, Willow hadn't yet managed to gain much real-world experience of the opposite sex.

Aside of a couple of summer residential stays, she had always lived at home, having studied garden design both online and through classes at the nearest college. Add in the work experience she had had to complete with a local landscape firm, the need to earn some money simply to eat while they had steadily fallen behind with the rent, the demands of her father's illness and his many medical appointments, and there hadn't been enough hours in the day for Willow to enjoy a social life with her friends as well. Gradually most of her friends had dropped away, but Shelley had been in her life since primary school and had continued to visit, oblivious to Brian Allerton's cool, snobbish attitude to her.

Willow arrived back at the tiny terraced house and she put on the kettle while Shelley set out the drinks and a solitary tray of shortbread. Just as Jai arrived, the vicar anxiously asked Willow where she was planning to move to.

'My sofa!' Shelley revealed with a chuckle. 'I wouldn't leave her stuck.'

'Yes, I'll be fine with Shelley until I can organise something more permanent. I have to move out of here tomorrow. The landlord has been wonderfully understanding but it would be selfish of me to stay here one day longer than necessary,' Willow explained, thinking that, tough though the last weeks had been, she *had* met with kindness in unexpected places.

A *sofa*? Willow was homeless? Expected to pack up and move in with a friend the same week that she had buried her father? Jai was appalled at that news. Honour demanded that he intervene but Willow had been raised to be proud and independent like her father and Jai would have to be sensitive in his approach. He was convinced that out of principle Willow would refuse his financial assistance.

'Coffee, Jai?' Willow prompted as she handed the vicar a cup of tea.

'Thank you,' he murmured, following her into the

small kitchen to say, 'Was your father at home at the end, or had he been moved to a hospice?'

'It was to happen next week,' Willow conceded tightly, throwing his tall dark figure a rueful appraisal, her heart giving a sudden thud as she collided involuntarily with ice-blue eyes enhanced by wondrously dense black lashes. 'But he didn't make it. His heart gave out.'

In an abrupt movement, she stepped back from him, disturbingly conscious of his height and the proximity of more masculinity than she felt able to bear. The very faint scent of some designer cologne drifted into her nostrils and she sucked in a sudden steadying breath, her level of awareness heightening exponentially to add to her discomfiture. She could feel her face heating, her knees wobbling as her tension rose even higher.

'What are you planning to do next?' Jai enquired, shifting his attention hurriedly from her lush pink lips and the X-rated images bombarding him while he questioned his behaviour.

Yes, she was indisputably beautiful, but he was neither a hormonal schoolboy, nor a sex-starved one, and he was challenged to explain his lack of self-discipline in her radius. She did, however, possess a quality that was exclusively her own, he acknowledged grudgingly, a slow-burning sensual appeal that

tugged hard at his senses. It was there in the flicker
of her languorous emerald eyes, the slight curve of
her generous lower lip, the upward angle of challenge
in her chin as she tilted her head back, strawberry-
blond hair falling in waves tumbling across her slim
shoulders like a swathe of rumpled silk.

'I'll be fine as soon as I find full-time work. These
last weeks, I was only able to work part-time hours.
Once I've saved up some money, I'll move on and
leave Shelley in peace.' She opened the fridge to ex-
tract milk and Jai noticed its empty interior.

'You have no food,' he remarked grimly.

'I genuinely haven't had much of an appetite recently,' she confided truthfully. 'And Dad ate next
to nothing, so I haven't been cooking.'

She had removed her coat and the simple grey
dress she wore hung loose on her slender body. Her
cheekbones were sharp, her eyes hollow and his misgivings increased because she looked haunted and
frail. Of course, common sense warned him that
nursing her father would have sapped her energy
and left her at a low ebb. Certainly, she was vulnerable, but she was a young and healthy woman and she
would probably be fine. But *probably* wasn't quite
good enough to satisfy Jai. He would make his own
checks and in the short term he would do what he
could to make her future less insecure.

* * *

Willow watched Jai leave, a sinking tightening sensation inside her chest as it occurred to her that she would probably never see him again now that her father was gone. Why would she want to see him again anyway? she asked herself irritably. They were only casual acquaintances and calling him a friend would have been pushing that slight bond to the limits.

Shelley departed only under protest.

'Are you sure you're going to be OK alone here tonight?' the brunette pressed, unconvinced. 'I don't feel right leaving you on your own.'

'I'm going to have a bath and go to bed early. I'm exhausted,' Willow told her ruefully. 'But thanks for caring.'

The two women hugged on the doorstep and Shelley went on her way. Willow cleared away the glasses and left the kitchen immaculate before heading upstairs for her bath. First thing in the morning a local dealer was coming to clear the house contents and sell them. There wasn't much left because almost everything that could be sold had been sold off weeks earlier. Even so, her father's beloved books might be worth something, she thought hopefully, her teeth worrying at her lower lip as she anxiously recalled the rent still owing. It would be a weight off her mind if she could clear that debt because their landlord belonged to her church and she suspected that he had felt that he'd had no choice but to allow them to remain as tenants even though the rent was in arrears. The sooner he was reimbursed for his kindness, the happier she would be.

The bell shrilled while she was putting on her pyjamas and she groaned, snatching her robe off the back of the bathroom door to hurry barefoot down the steep stairs and answer the door.

When she saw Jai outside, she froze in disconcertion.

'I brought dinner,' Jai informed her as she hovered, her grip on the robe she was holding closed loosening to reveal the shorts and T-shirt she wore beneath and her long, shapely legs. He drew in a stark little breath as she stepped back and the robe shifted again to expose the tilted peaks of her small breasts. In a split second he was hard as a rock, his body impervious to his belief that he preferred curvier women.

'D-dinner?' she stammered in wonderment as Jai stepped back and two men with a trolley moved out from behind him and, with some difficulty, trundled the unwieldy item through the tiny hall into the cramped living room with its small table and two chairs.

Those wolf-blue eyes of his held her fast, all breathing in suspension.

'My hotel was able to provide us with an evening meal,' he clarified smoothly.

No takeaways for Jai, Willow registered without surprise while she wondered what on earth such an extravagant gesture could have cost him. Of course, he didn't have to count costs, did he? It probably hadn't even occurred to him that requesting a meal for two people that could be transported out of the hotel and served by hotel staff was an extraordinary request. Jai was simply accustomed to asking and always receiving, regardless of expense.

'I'm not dressed,' she said awkwardly, tightening the tie on her robe in an apologetic gesture.

'It doesn't bother me. We should eat now while it's still warm,' Jai responded as the plates were brought to the table, and she settled down opposite him, stiff with unease.

A bottle of wine was uncorked, glasses produced and set by their places.

'I thought you didn't drink,' she commented in surprise as the waiters went back outside again, presumably to wait for them to finish.

'I take wine with my meals,' he explained. 'It's rare for me to drink at any other time.'

His eyes had a ring of stormy grey around the pupils, she noted absently, her throat tightening as her gaze dropped to the fullness of his sensual lower lip and she found herself wondering for the first time ever what Jai would be like in bed. She had been too shy and immature for such thoughts when she was an infatuated teenager and, now that she was an adult, her mental audacity brought a flood of mortified colour to her pale cheeks. Would he be gentle or rough? Fiery or smoothly precise? Her thoughts refused to quit.

'Why did you feel that you had to feed me?' she asked abruptly in an effort to deflect his attention from her hot cheeks.

'You had no food in the kitchen. You've just lost your father,' Jai parried calmly as he began to eat. 'I didn't like to think of you alone here.'

He had felt sorry for her. She busied herself eating the delicious food, striving not to squirm with mortification that she had impressed him as an object of pity. After all, Jai had been raised by his benevolent father to constantly consider those less fortunate and now ran a huge international charity devoted to good causes. Whether she appreciated the reality or not, looking out for the needs of the vulnerable had to come as naturally to Jai as breathing.

'Why are you moving out of here tomorrow?' he pressed quietly.

Willow snatched in a long steadying breath and then surrendered to the inevitable, reasoning that her father could no longer be humiliated by the truth. She explained about Brian Allerton's unsuccessful stock-market dealing and the impoverishment that had followed. 'I mean no disrespect,' she completed ruefully, 'but my father was irresponsible with money. He never saved anything—he only had his pension. All his working life he lived in accommodation provided by his employers and most of his meals and bills were also covered and it didn't prepare him very well for retirement living in the normal world.'

'That didn't occur to me, but it should've done,' Jai conceded. 'He was an unworldly man.'

'He was so ashamed of his financial losses,' she whispered unhappily. 'It made him feel like a failure and that's one of the reasons he wouldn't see people any more.'

'I wish he had found it possible to reach out to me for assistance,' Jai framed heavily, his lean, strong face clenched hard. 'So, you are being forced to sell everything? I will buy his book collection.'

Willow stared across the table at him in shock. *'Seriously?'*

'He was a lifelong book collector, as am I,' Jai pointed out. 'I would purchase his books because I want them and for no other reason. We will agree that tonight and hopefully that will take care of your rent arrears.'

Willow nodded slowly and then frowned. 'Are you sure you want them?'

'I have a library in every one of my homes. Of course, I want them.'

Willow swallowed hard. 'How many homes do you have?' she whispered helplessly.

'More than I want in Chandrapur but it is my duty, as it was my father's, to preserve our heritage properties for future generations,' he countered levelly. 'Now let us move on to other, more important matters. Your father was too proud to ask for my help. I hope you are a little more sensible.'

Reckoning that he was about to embarrass her by offering her further financial help, Willow pushed back her plate and stood up to forestall him. 'I'm going upstairs to get dressed first,' she said tightly.

Jai sipped his wine and signalled the staff to remove the dishes and the trolley. He pictured Willow sliding out of the robe, letting it fall sinuously to her feet before she took off the top and removed the shorts. His imagination went wild while he did so, his body surging with fierce hunger, and he gritted his teeth angrily, struggling to get his thoughts back in his control.

Upstairs, Willow stood immobile, reckoning that

Jai taking her father's books could well settle the rent arrears. Did he really want those books? Or was that just a ploy to give her money? And when someone was as poor as she was, could she really afford to worry about what might lie behind his generosity?

Her attention fell on a sapphire ring that lay on the tray on the dressing table. It was her grandmother's engagement ring and it would have to be sold too, even though it was unlikely to be worth very much. Her father had refused to let her sell it while he was still alive, but it had to go now, along with everything else. She could not live with Shelley without paying her way. She would not take advantage of her friend's kindness like that.

She spread a glance round the room, her eyes lingering on the precious childhood items that would also have to be disposed of, things like her worn teddy bear and the silver frame housing a photo of the mother she barely remembered. She couldn't lug boxes of stuff with her to clutter up Shelley's small studio apartment. Be practical, Willow, she scolded herself even as a sob of pain convulsed her throat.

She felt as though her whole life had tumbled into broken pieces at her feet. Her father was gone. Everything familiar was fading. And at the heart of her grief lay the inescapable truth that she had *always* been a serious disappointment to the father she loved.

No matter how hard she had tried, no matter how many tutors her father had engaged to coach her, she had continually failed to reach the academic heights he'd craved for his only child. She wasn't stupid, she was merely average, and to a man as clever as her father had been, a man with a string of Oxford degrees in excellence, that had been a cruel punishment...

Downstairs, enjoying a second glass of wine, Jai heard her choked sob. He squared his shoulders and breathed in deep, deeming it only natural that at some point on such a day Willow's control would weaken and she would break down. There had been no visible tears at the funeral, no emotional conversations afterwards that he had heard. Throughout, Willow had been polite and pleasant and more considerate of other people's feelings than her own. She had attempted to bring an upbeat note to a depressing situation, had behaved as though she had already completely accepted the changes that her father's death would inflict on her.

When the sounds of her distress became more than he could withstand, Jai abandoned his careful scrutiny of her father's books—several first editions, he noted with satisfaction, worthy of the fine price he would pay for them. He drained his glass and forced himself to mount the stairs to offer what comfort he could. All too well did he remember that he himself had had little support after his father's sudden death from a massive stroke. Thousands had been devastated by the passing of so well-loved a figure and hundreds of concerned relatives had converged on Jai to share his sorrow, but Jai hadn't been close enough to any of those individuals to find solace in their memories. In reality only *he* had known his father on a very personal, private level and only *he* could know the extent of the loss he had sustained.

Willow was lying sobbing on the bed and Jai didn't hesitate. He sat down beside her and lifted her into his arms, reckoning that she weighed barely more than a child and instinctively treating her as such as he patted her slender spine soothingly and struggled to think of what it was best to say. 'Remember the good times with your father,' he urged softly.

'There really *weren't* any...' Willow muttered chokily into his shoulder, startled to find herself in his arms but revelling in that sudden comforting closeness of another human being and no longer feeling alone and adrift. 'I was always a serious disappointment to him.'

With a frown of disbelief, Jai held her back from him to look down into her tear-stained face. The tip of her nose was red, which was surprisingly cute.

Her wide green eyes were still welling with tears and oddly defiant, as if daring him to disagree. 'How could that possibly be true?' he challenged.

'I didn't do well enough at school, didn't get into the *right* schools either,' Willow confided shakily, looking into his lean, strong face and those commanding ice-blue eyes that had once haunted her dreams. 'Once I heard him lying to make excuses for me. He told one of his colleagues that I'd been ill when I sat my exams and it *was* a lie… Dad wanted a child he could brag about, an intellectual child, who passed every exam with flying colours. I had tutors in every subject and I *still* couldn't do well enough to please him!'

Jai was sharply disconcerted by that emotional admission, which revealed a far less agreeable side to a man he had both liked and respected. 'I'm sure he didn't mean to make you feel that way,' he began tentatively.

Willow's fingers clenched for support into a broad shoulder that felt reassuringly solid and strong and she sucked in a shuddering breath. It was a kind lie, she conceded, liking him all the more for his compassion. Even so, she was still keen to say what she had never had the nerve to say before, because only then, in getting it off her chest, might she start to heal from the low self-esteem she had long suffered from. 'Yes, Dad did mean it. He honestly believed that the harder he pushed me, the more chance he had of getting me to excel! He didn't even care about which subject it might be in, he just wanted me to be especially talented at *something*!'

'I'm sorry,' Jai breathed, mesmerised by the glistening depth of her green eyes and the sheer passion with which she spoke, not to mention the unexpected pleasure of the slight trusting weight of her lying across his thighs and the evocative coconut scent of her hair. The untimely throb of arousal at his groin infuriated him and he fought it to the last ditch.

'Dad wasn't remotely impressed by my studying garden history and landscaping. And that's why I'm crying, because I'm sorry too that it's too late to change anything for the better. I had my chance with him, and I blew it!' Willow muttered guiltily, marvelling that she was confiding in Jai, of all people. Jai, who was the cleverest of the clever. It didn't feel real; it felt much more like something she would imagine to comfort herself and, as such, reassuringly unreal and harmless. 'I never once managed to do anything that made Dad proud of me. My small successes were never enough to please him.'

And the sheer honesty of that confession struck Jai on a much deeper level because he wasn't used to a woman who told it as it was and didn't wrap up the ugly truth in a flattering guise. Yet Willow looked back at him, fearless and frank and so, *so* sad, and his hands slid from her back up to her face to cup her cheekbones, framing those dreamy green eyes that had so much depth and eloquence in her heart-shaped face. She looked impossibly beautiful.

He didn't know what to say to that. He did not want to criticise her father, he did not want to hurt her more, and so he kissed her…didn't even know he was going to do it, didn't even have to think about it because it seemed the utterly, absolutely natural next step in their new understanding.

CHAPTER TWO

THE TASTE OF JAI, of fine wine and a faint minty after-flavour, threw Willow even deeper into the realms of fantasy.

Because fantasy was what it felt like, totally unthreatening fantasy in which Prince Jai Hari Singh, Maharaja of Chandrapur, kissed *her*, Willow Allerton, currently unemployed and soon to be homeless into the bargain. Being in his arms didn't feel real but, goodness, it felt *good*, the delve of his tongue into the moist aperture of her mouth sending a shower of fireworks flying through her tummy, awakening a heat that surged enthusiastically into all the cold places inside her, both comforting and exhilarating all at once.

It was everything she had dreamt she might find in a man's arms and it felt right as well as good, gloriously right as if she had been waiting her whole life for that moment and was being richly rewarded for her patience. In the dim light from the bedside lamp, Jai's eyes glittered with the pale ice of polar stars, but the ice that powered him burned through her like a rejuvenating drug, banishing the grief and the guilt and the sadness that had filled her to overflowing. Her fingers drifted up to curve to his strong jawline.

'I like this,' she whispered helplessly.

'I like it too much,' Jai conceded in a driven undertone, lifting her off his lap to lay her down on the bed where her strawberry-blond hair shone in the lamplight, leaning over her to cover her lush mouth with his again.

'How...*too much*?' she pressed.

'I was trying to comfort you, not—'

Featherlight fingers brushed his lips before he could complete that speech. 'Kiss me again,' she urged feverishly. 'It drives everything else out of my head.'

She wanted forgetfulness, not the down-to-earth reminder that such intimacy was untimely. Jai's stern cautious side warred with his libido, his body teeming with pent-up desire. They were alone and free-to-consent adults, not irresponsible teenagers. He gazed down at her and then wrenched at the constriction of his tie with an impatient hand, suddenly giving way to the passionate nature that he usually controlled to what he deemed an acceptable level. The allure of her pink ripe lips was more than he could withstand.

That next explosive kiss sealed Willow's fate, for she could no more have denied the hunger coursing through her than she could have denied her own name. There was also a strong element of wonder in discovering Jai's desire for her. That was thrillingly unexpected and wonderfully heartening, that she could have it within her to mysteriously attract a man well known for his preference for gorgeous models and Bollywood actresses, a gorgeous, incredibly sexy man, who could have had virtually any woman he wanted. It changed her view of herself as the girl next door, low on sex appeal.

'I want you,' Jai ground out against her reddened mouth as he shed his jacket with a lithe twist of his broad shoulders.

Only for a split second did she marvel at that and then all her insecurities surged to the fore because she was skinny and lacked the curves that were so often seen as essential to make a woman appealing to a man. But an internal voice reminded her that Jai wanted her, and she opened her mouth beneath the onslaught of his, let her tongue dart and tangle with his, feeling free, feeling daring for the first time ever.

There was intoxication in the demanding pressure of his mouth on hers and the long fingers sliding below her top to cup a small pouting breast while he toyed with the tender peak. Her body arched without her volition as that sensual caress grew more intense, tiny little arrows of heat darting down into her pelvis to make her extraordinarily aware of that area. Her hips shifted as he pulled her top off, exposing the bare swell of her breasts, bending over her to use his mouth on the plump pink nipples commanding his attention. She tingled all over, goose bumps rising on her arms as he suckled on the distended buds. Between her thighs she felt hot and damp and surprisingly impatient for what came next.

And she knew what came next, of course she did, but her friends' bluntness on the topic had warned her not to expect triumphant bursts of classical music and glimpses of heaven in the final stages. It would be her first time and she was aware that her lack of experience would not affect his enjoyment but that it might well detract from hers. All a matter of luck, a friend had told her sagely.

Dainty fingers spearing through Jai's silky black hair, Willow was revelling in the intimacy of being able to touch him while still marvelling over how fast things could change between two people. Yet she had no doubts and was convinced she would have no regrets either because she had already reached the conclusion that she would rather have Jai as her first lover than anyone else.

Jai dragged off his shirt, returned to kiss her again, his wide, powerful torso hard and muscular against hers. She made a little sound of appreciation deep in her throat even as her hands skated up the hot, smooth skin of his ribcage to discover the muscles that flexed with his every movement. She couldn't think any more beyond that moment because the craving he had unleashed grew stronger with every demanding kiss and utterly controlled her, dulling her brain with an adrenalin boost that was wholly physical.

She writhed under his weight as he traced the hot, swollen centre of her, touching her where she desperately needed to be touched so that her body arched up to him, her heartbeat thundering, her entire being quivering with feverish need. A finger penetrated her slick depths and she gasped, all arousal and captive energy, wanting, *wanting*...

'Is it safe?' Jai husked, wrenching at his trousers to get them out of his path and so overexcited he barely recognised himself in his eagerness but her response, the passage of her tiny hands smoothing over his overheated body, had pushed him to the biting edge of a hunger greater than anything he had ever known before.

Safe? *Safe?* What was he talking about? She wasn't expecting any more visitors; they were alone. Of course, they were safe from interruption or the potential embarrassment of discovery.

'Of course, it is,' Willow muttered.

Jai came down to her with a wolfish smile of relief. 'How very fortunate... I don't think I could stop unless you ordered me to.'

'Not going to,' Willow mumbled, entranced by the fierce black-fringed eyes above hers into absolute stillness.

Jai tipped her legs back and slid sinuously between them, shifting forward in a forceful surge to plunge into her. Eyes closing, Willow felt the burn of his invasion as her untried body stretched to accommodate him and then a sharp stab of pain that jolted her even as he groaned with satisfaction.

'You're so tight,' he breathed appreciatively.

The pain faded and, as it had been less than she had feared, her stress level dropped, and her body relaxed to rise up against his as he withdrew and forged back into her again. Little tendrils of warming sensation gathered in her pelvis and the excitement flooded back, kicking up her heartrate simultaneously so that even breathing became a challenge. She moved against him, hot, damp with perspiration, losing control because the insidious tightening at her core stoked her hunger for him. His fluid insistent rhythm increased, and she felt frantic, pitched to an edge of need that felt unbearable. She lifted to meet his every thrust, need driving her to hasten to the finish line and then, with a swoosh of drowning sensation, the tightness transformed into an explosion of sheer pleasure unlike any she had ever envisaged and she fell back against the pillows, winded and drained, utterly incapable of even twitching a limb.

'That was incredible,' Jai purred like a well-fed jungle cat in her ear, long fingers tracing the relaxed pout of her mouth and trailing down to her shoulder to smooth the skin before he pressed his mouth hungrily to the slope of her neck. 'All I really want now is to do it all over again.'

The tension of discomfiture, of not knowing how to behave, beginning to rise in Willow ebbed. He was happy, *she* was happy, there was nothing to fret about. *Again*, though? She had assumed that men were once-only creatures in need of recovery time, but Jai was already shifting sensually against her again, his renewed arousal brushing her stomach. That he could still want her that much gratified her and she smiled up at him.

That smile full of sunshine disconcerted Jai. His conscience twinged and it took him a moment to recognise the unfamiliar prompting because it was rare for him to do anything that awakened such a reaction. 'You do realise that this…*us*, isn't likely to go anywhere?' he murmured.

'How could it? I'm not an idiot,' Willow parried in surprise and embarrassment that he felt the need to tell her that they had no future as a couple.

'I didn't want you to get the wrong impression,' Jai told her levelly. 'I only do casual with women and I never raise expectations I have no plans to fulfil.'

'Neither do I,' Willow assured him cheerfully, secure in her conviction that he had not guessed that she was inexperienced and relieved because pride demanded that he believe that he was no big deal in her life. 'I wouldn't want you getting the wrong idea about me either.'

Faint colour edged Jai's high sculpted cheekbones because no woman had ever dared to tell *him* that he was just a casual encounter. 'Of course not.'

'Then we're both content,' Willow concluded, refusing to recognise the little pang of hurt buried deep within her…hurt that she wasn't a little different from other women in his eyes, more special than they were, somehow less of a casual event in his life. He was telling it as it was and she should be grateful for that. This way she knew exactly where she stood and she wouldn't be weaving fantasies around phone calls that would never come or surprise visits. After all, he didn't have her phone number and even she didn't know where she'd eventually be living. She and Jai really *were* ships that passed in the night.

'I want to kiss you again,' Jai breathed with a raw edge to his dark deep voice.

He had only one night with her, and he wanted to make the very most of the best sex he had ever had. He would move on; she would move on. That was the way of the world, yet a stray shard of guilt and regret still pierced him because she was so open with him, so impervious to his wealth and status. He would check that she was all right from a safe distance, stay uninvolved, he promised himself. He supposed there *were* ties between them that he was refusing to acknowledge lest they make him uncomfortable. He had vague memories of her as a child, could remember her shouting his name in excitement at sports events and could recall the way her eyes had once clung to him as though magnetised. But she had grown out of all that. Of course, she had.

'I'm cold,' Willow admitted, snaking back from him to tug the edge of the duvet up and scramble under it with a convulsive shiver.

Jai peeled off his trousers, shaken that in his haste to possess her he had not even fully undressed. Nothing cool or sophisticated about that approach, he told himself ruefully, wondering what it was about her that had made him so downright desperate to have her. For the first time with a woman sexual hunger had overwhelmed him and crowded every other consideration out. It was something more than looks, maybe that unspoiled natural quality of hers, not to mention her disconcerting honesty in assuring him that he was just a one-night stand and that she had no desire to attach strings to him. Jai didn't think he had ever been with a woman who *didn't* want those strings, no matter how coolly she was trying to play the game. He was too rich and too powerful not to inspire women with ambitious hopes and plans.

'Let me warm you,' Jai urged, hauling her into contact with his hot, muscular length, driving out the shivers that had been assailing her.

And it all began again and this time she was wholly free of tension and insecurity and the excitement rose even faster for her. The pleasure stole her mind from her body and left her exhausted. She dropped into sleep, still melded to Jai and still amazed by what had happened between them. At some stage of the night he kissed her awake and made love to her again, slow and sure this time, and achingly sexy. It occurred to her that Jai had made her initiation into sex wondrously sensual but, even then, she knew she ached in bone and muscle and would be wrecked the next morning.

In the dull light of dawn, she was surprised when Jai shook her awake. Dressed in his dark suit and unshaven, he stood over her, studying her with wolf pale blue eyes that burned. He yanked back the duvet, rudely exposing her, and said roughly, 'There's blood all over the sheet! Did I hurt you?'

Willow wanted to die of humiliation where she sat and she snatched at the duvet in desperation and covered up the offending stain, her face burning as hot as a furnace. 'Of course, you didn't. I didn't realise I would bleed the first time,' she whispered shakily. 'I know some women do but somehow I assumed I wouldn't...'

Slow, painful comprehension gripped Jai and rocked him to the depths of his being. He stared down at her in dawning disbelief. 'Are you saying that you were a virgin?'

'Well, it's not something I can lie about now, is it?' Willow muttered in embarrassment, her chin coming up at a defiant tilt. 'But I don't know why you would think that you have a right to make a production out of something that is my business and nothing to do with you.'

'I would not have chosen to sleep with you had I known I would be your first,' Jai framed fiercely.

'Well, if that was a personal concern of yours,

you should've asked in advance,' Willow countered mutinously. 'It's not as if I dragged you into bed!'

'How the hell could I have guessed that you were still a virgin at your age?' Jai demanded.

'I'm only twenty-one. Twenty-two in a few months,' she added stiffly. 'I'm sure I'm not that unusual.'

Jai was not appeased. She was years younger than the women he usually took as lovers, but he hadn't registered that fact the night before, had been too turned on and in too much of a hurry to register anything important, he conceded, angry at his own recklessness.

'Perhaps not, but I assumed you were experienced,' he admitted flatly.

'Well, now you know different. Can we drop this discussion? I want to get washed and dressed,' Willow told him without any expression at all, her small, slight body rigid with wounded pride and resentment in the bed as she continued to hug the duvet to her. 'You know last night was lovely…but now you've ruined it.'

'I'll see you downstairs,' Jai countered grimly.

Willow scrambled out of bed as soon as the door closed behind him and then winced, her body letting her know that such sudden energetic movements would be punished. Just at that moment she did not want that reminder of the intimacy they had shared when Jai, so obviously, regretted it. She pulled out fresh clothing and trekked across to the small shower room. A damp towel lay on the floor and she bent to scoop it up and lift it to her nose. It smelled ever so faintly of Jai while her body smelled even more strongly of him. Shame engulfed her in a drowning flood of regret. Evidently in sleeping with him she had made the wrong decision, but surely it had been *her* decision to make?

Of course, there had been men who'd shown an interest in her in recent years, but none had attracted her enough for her to take matters any further. She had never been much of a fan of crowded clubs or parties and her father's demand that she come home at a reasonable hour had proved to be a restriction that had turned her into a deadbeat companion for a night out. She had taken the easy way out when faced with her father's domineering personality and she had spent her free evenings at home watching television and catching up with Shelley, none of which had given her any experience of how to handle Jai in a temper. But never again would she lie down to be walked over by an angry male, she told herself urgently. From now on she would stand her ground and hold her head high, even if she did have misgivings about her own behaviour.

* * *

Jai paced the small living room, feeling the claustro-phobic proportions of its confines in growing frustration. Willow was twenty-one years old. Far too young for an experienced man of twenty-nine. Why hadn't he remembered how young she was? What had he been thinking of? The answer was that he *hadn't* been thinking, hadn't stopped to think *once*. Everything that had happened with Willow had happened so fast and had seemed so deceptively natural that he had questioned nothing and now it was too late to change anything.

'Last night was lovely...but now you've ruined it.'

That complaint, towering in its naivety, echoed in his ears and made him flinch. As a rule, he avoided starry-eyed girls and she was one he should definitely have avoided getting more deeply involved with. A woman who'd had a massive crush on him as a teenager? How much had that influenced her willingness to give him her body? He emitted a harsh groan of guilt and self-loathing.

A decent man didn't take advantage of a vulnerable woman! And what had he done?

Within hours of her father's funeral, when she was grieving and distressed, he had pounced like some sort of self-serving seducer. She had deserved more care and consideration than he had given her. Yet he had started out simply trying to offer both care and consideration and could not for the life of him explain how trying to comfort her had ended up with them having sex. She hadn't flirted with him. She hadn't encouraged him but she hadn't said no either. Was that what he was blaming her for? No, he was blaming her for not telling him that she was a virgin, for not giving him that choice…

'I'll have to nip out to get something for breakfast,' Willow told him from the doorway.

Jai swung round, his eyes a pale glittering brilliance in his lean, darkly handsome face. 'I'll eat back at the hotel,' he told her drily. 'Why didn't you tell me that I would be the first? I wouldn't have continued if I'd known. I feel as though I took advantage of your inexperience.'

'It didn't occur to me that I should tell you. I wasn't really thinking. I don't think either of us were. Everything happened so fast,' Willow murmured defensively, wishing he would have given her the time to provide breakfast and sort matters out in a more civilised manner. But Jai, she was beginning to recognise, was much more volatile in nature than she had ever appreciated. Without skipping a beat, he had taken the dialogue they had abandoned in the bedroom straight back up again, which suggested that while she'd showered and dressed, he had merely continued to silently brood and seethe.

'There's nothing we can do about it now,' she pointed out thinly.

Jai looked back at her, scanning her small, slight figure in jeans and a top. Even with the shadows etched below her eyes, she was still lovely, eminently touchable, he reflected as he tensed. Daylight and cold reason had not made her any less appealing. 'No, but it was *wrong.*'

'You don't get the unilateral right to say that to me,' Willow snapped back at him. 'It was *not* wrong for me!'

'You had a crush on me for years,' Jai countered levelly. 'Is that why it wasn't wrong for you?'

Willow's soft mouth opened and closed again as she gazed back at him in horror, hot, painful colour slowly washing up her cheeks. 'I can't believe you are throwing that in my face.'

'It's relevant to this situation,' Jai breathed sardonically.

'The only person making a situation out of this is you!' Willow condemned, fighting her mortification with all her might. 'Yes, I may have had a crush on you when I was a schoolgirl, but I grew out of that nonsense years ago!'

'I'm not sure I can believe that some sentimental memory didn't influence you.'

'It didn't. Whether you believe that or not is up to you,' Willow replied curtly. 'I'm all grown up now. I don't have any romantic notions about you...and if I had, you'd have killed them stone dead.'

Her continuing refusal to be influenced by his attitude surprised Jai. He was accustomed to those he dealt with coming round to his view and supporting his opinion, but Willow was stubborn enough and independent enough not to budge an inch. Meanwhile those bright green eyes, reminiscent of fresh ferns in the shade, damned him to hell and back.

'Then let's get down to business,' Jai suggested, disconcerting her when she was bracing herself for another round of the same conversation. 'I want to buy your father's books.'

Willow regrouped and contrived to nod. 'I'm content with that.'

'Is the dealer you mentioned last night a book dealer?'

'Nothing so fancy...why?'

'At least two of the books are quite valuable first editions and you could do better auctioning them,' Jai warned.

'I haven't time for that. I didn't know any of them would be worth anything,' she completed stiffly.

'I will buy them at a fair price but you may wish to take further advice.'

Willow groaned out loud. 'Oh, Jai… I don't think you're likely to cheat me!'

'Very well. The books will be packed for you and collected later this morning and I will pay you in cash as that may be more convenient for you right now,' Jai murmured levelly. 'Will you allow me to pay for you to stay in a hotel until you get on your feet again?'

'Would you be offering me that option if you hadn't slept with me last night?' Willow asked suspiciously.

His eyes clashed with her sceptical appraisal. 'Yes.'

'No. Thanks, but no,' Willow told him without hesitation. 'I don't mind staying with Shelley for a while.'

'Will you accept any further assistance from me?' Jai enquired.

'I'd prefer not to,' Willow responded truthfully.

'Life isn't always that straightforward,' Jai replied wryly as he settled his business card on the table. 'If at any time you need help, you can depend on me to deliver it, no strings attached. Phone me if you are in need.'

'And why would you make me an offer like that?' Willow demanded shortly.

'I wish you well,' Jai admitted levelly.

Willow spun around in a rather ungainly circle and went to open the front door. 'I'll get by fine without you,' she told him with a defiantly bright smile. 'But thanks for caring.'

And on that hollow note, Jai departed. As soon as he was gone, Willow felt empty, exhausted and horribly hurt. She would never see him again except in newspapers or magazines at some glamorous or important event, but that was for the best because Jai had rejected her on every level. He had switched back to treating her like a distant acquaintance, whom he was willing to help in times of trouble, smoothly distancing himself from their brief intimacy.

He not only regretted sleeping with her, but also suspected that she had slept with him because she had once been infatuated with him. He had made mincemeat out of her pride and humiliated her.

Goodbye, Jai, she thought numbly. *Goodbye and good riddance!*

CHAPTER THREE

WILLOW SAT ON the side of the bath and waited for the wand to give her a result while Shelley sidled round the door, too impatient to wait outside. 'Well?' she pressed excitedly.

'Another thirty seconds,' Willow muttered wearily.

'I love babies.' Shelley sighed dreamily.

'So do I… I just thought it would be years before I had one. And maybe it will be,' Willow contended, trying not to be too pessimistic.

After all, skipping a period wasn't always a sign of pregnancy even in a woman with a regular cycle. But then there was also the soreness of her breasts, the occasional light-headed sensation and her sudden sensitivity to smells and tastes that had never bothered her before. Yet Willow still couldn't credit that an unplanned pregnancy could happen to her. Surely Jai had used condoms? She hadn't thought to check or ask him, had simply not even considered the danger of conception, which had been exceedingly foolish when it was she who would fall pregnant if anything went amiss. Maybe a condom had failed, maybe during the night he had forgotten to use one, maybe she was just one of the unfortunate few who conceived regardless of the contraception used.

'Congratulations!' Shelley carolled irrepressibly and grabbed her into an enthusiastic hug. 'You're pregnant.'

Willow paled. 'Are you sure?' she gasped, peering down at the wand for herself, and there it was: the line for a positive result.

'You'll have to go to the doctor ASAP,' Shelley warned her. 'I mean…you must be at least eight weeks along now and you should be taking vitamins and stuff.'

In no hurry to approach a doctor for confirmation, Willow wandered back out to the very comfortable sofa she slept on and sank heavily down. *Pregnant!* Just when her life was slowly beginning to settle again into a new routine, fate had thrown her onto a roller coaster of a ride that would destroy all her self-improvement plans. Of course, there were options other than keeping the baby to raise, she reminded herself doggedly, even while she knew that neither termination nor adoption had any appeal for her.

But how on earth would she manage? Currently

she was waitressing in the bar that Shelley managed. The tips were good, particularly at weekends, and in another couple of months she would have saved up enough for a deposit for a little place of her own. After making that move, she had planned to polish up her CV and start trying to find work in the landscaping field that would pay enough for her to live on. She had her qualification now and even the most junior position would be a good start to a decent career and perhaps, ultimately, her own business. Throw a baby into the midst of those plans, however, and it blew them all to smithereens!

And yet the prospect of having Jai's baby was already beginning to warm her at some deep level, although she felt guilty about feeling that way. He mightn't have wanted her, but he couldn't prevent her from having his child and she did love babies, and the thought of one of her own pleased and frightened her in equal parts. She didn't have a single relative left alive, but her baby could be the foundation of a new family, she reflected lovingly.

She had lain awake on the sofa many nights reliving that night with Jai, wishing she didn't feel like such an immature idiot for having slept with him in the first place and wishing that she didn't miss him now that he was gone again. She wasn't kidding herself that she was in love with him or anything like that, but she could not deny that Jai, the Maharaja of Chandrapur, had always fascinated her and that he had attracted her more powerfully than anyone else ever had. Those were the facts and she tried not to dress them up. She felt that she should've called a halt to their intimacy, but she hadn't and the coolness of his departure had been her punishment. He had hurt her, but she tried not to dwell on those wounded feelings because what would be the point in indulging herself in such sad thoughts?

'I'll help you every step of the way,' Shelley told her, sitting down beside her to grip her hand comfortingly. 'We'll get through it together…and at least you won't have to worry about money, not with the father being rich.'

'I'm *not* going to tell Jai!' Willow exclaimed in dismay. 'He didn't want me so he's even less likely to want a baby with me!'

'It takes two to tango.'

'And one to have common sense, and neither of us had any that night.' Willow sighed and then groaned out loud. 'Why should I make him suffer too? It would be so humiliating as well. I can't face that on top of everything else.'

Shelley's freckled face and bright blue eyes were troubled below her mop of brown curls. 'Well, then, what are you planning to do?'

'I don't want to tell Jai… To be frank, I don't want anything more to do with him,' Willow admitted unhappily. 'I'll work this out without bothering him for help. Somehow I'll work it out even if it means living on welfare benefits to survive.'

Two weeks later, while Willow was at work, Shelley had to deal with the surprise of Jai himself turning up on the doorstep asking after Willow because he hadn't heard from her. Aware that her friend wanted no further contact with him, Shelley lied and said that Willow had moved out and hadn't yet sent her a forwarding address. Jai left his mobile number with her.

Thirteen months later, the private investigation agency Jai had hired to find Willow finally tracked her down and, in the midst of his working day in his London office, Jai immediately settled down with a sense of urgency to flick open the ominously slim file.

The first fact he learned was that the investigation team had only contrived to find Willow by covertly watching and following her friend, Shelley. Jai was disconcerted to learn that Willow's friend had lied to him when he had only had Willow's best interests in mind. He would have been satisfied with the assurance that she was safe and well. He assumed

that Willow had confided in her friend and it was
conceivable that that night he had spent with her had
muddied the water in her friend's eyes and made his
motivations seem more questionable, he conceded
grudgingly.

After all, what could Willow possibly have to hide
from him? Why would she get lost and neglect to get
in touch with him when he had been so specific on
that point? Had he offended her to such an extent?

He knew he had not been tactful. He had been
too outspoken. He had embarrassed her, hurt her, he
recalled unhappily. But he had been very shocked
to realise that he had taken advantage of her inno-
cence and his self-loathing on that score had still to
fade, as had his recollections of that night. It seemed
even worse to him that the memories of her still remained so fresh. Averse as he now was to any kind
of casual encounter, he had not been with a woman
since then. He had broken his own code of honour
unforgettably with Willow and had buried himself
in work while struggling to come to terms with that
depressing truth.

Her disappearance and continuing silence had seriously worried him and had only made him even
more determined to locate her.

The bald facts of what came next in the file shook
Jai to his essentially conservative core and he was

instantly grateful that he had refused to give up on his search for her because she was in trouble. Willow had had a child and was now living in a hostel for the homeless, waiting for the local council to find her more suitable accommodation. A *child*? How was that possible in so short a time frame? Had she turned to some other man for comfort after he had left her? He focussed back on the printed page and his blood ran cold in his veins when he saw the birthdate of the child and then, startlingly, his own middle *name*... Hari.

Far across London, Willow knelt on the floorboards while Hari sat on his little blanket and mouthed the plastic ball he was playing with. Everything went into his mouth and she had to watch him like a hawk. He was almost seven months old and, although he couldn't yet crawl, he had discovered that he could get around very nicely just by rolling over and over so that he could get his little chubby hands on anything that attracted his attention. And *everything* attracted Hari's attention, which meant that she needed eyes in the back of her head to keep him safe.

She had not known that it was possible to love anyone as much as she loved Hari. Her love for the father she had continually failed to please paled in comparison. From the moment Hari had arrived he had become her world and she was painfully conscious that as a mother she had nothing to offer in material terms. Sadly, moving into the hostel had been a necessity to get on the housing list. Shelley hadn't wanted them to move out of her apartment but staying any longer hadn't been an option in the chaos that she and Hari had brought to her friend's life. So she might be, for the moment, a less than stellar mother to her son, but in time she would get better and provide him with a decent home where their life would improve.

The knock that sounded on the door made her jump and she peered through the peephole to identify another resident, the woman from the room next to hers, before she undid the lock.

'Reception asked me to tell you that you have a visitor waiting down in the basement,' the woman told her.

Willow suppressed a sigh and bundled Hari, his blanket and a couple of toys up into her arms. Visitors weren't allowed to enter the rooms in the hostel, but the basement was available for necessary meetings with housing officials, social workers and counsellors. Willow hadn't been expecting anyone, but the number of people now involved in checking up on her and Hari and asking her to fill in forms seemed never-ending.

My goodness, maybe somewhere had finally been found for her and Hari to live, she thought optimisti-

cally as she walked down the steps to the basement
to enter a large grey-painted room furnished mainly
with small tables and chairs, few of which were occupied. She hovered in the doorway and then froze
when she saw Jai standing by the barred window
that overlooked a dark alleyway.

Jai looked so incredibly out of place against such
a backdrop that she could not quite believe her eyes
and she blinked rapidly. Clad in a black pinstriped
suit teamed with a white shirt and gold tie, he looked
incredibly intimidating. But he also looked impossibly exclusive and gorgeous with that suit sharply
tailored to a perfect fit over his tall, powerful frame.
The stark lighting above, which flattered no one,
somehow still contrived to flatter Jai, enhancing the
golden glow of his skin and the blue-black luxuri-
ance of his hair and accentuating the proud sculpted
lines and hollows of his superb bone structure. He
was stunning as he stood there, absolutely stunning,
his light eyes glittering in his lean, strong face, and
she swallowed convulsively, wondering how he had
found her, what he wanted with her and how on earth
she could possibly hide Hari from him when she was
holding him in her arms.

Jai noticed Willow at almost the same moment,
lodged across the room, a tiny frail figure dressed

in jeans and an oversized sweater, against which she held a child. And he stared at the child in her arms with helpless intensity and, even at that distance, he recognised his son in the baby's olive-toned skin and black hair. His *son*... Jai could not work out how that was possible unless Willow had lied to him about it being safe for them to make love without him taking additional precautions. But just at that moment the *how* seemed less significant than the overpowering and breathtaking sense of recognition that gripped him when he glimpsed his infant son for the first time.

Willow walked towards him and he strode forward to greet her, noticing that she was struggling to carry the child along with the other things she held. Without hesitation, Jai extended his hands and lifted the baby right out of her arms.

Hari chortled and smiled up at him. Evidently, he was a happy baby, who delighted in new faces. Jai looked into eyes as pale a blue as his own, his sole inheritance from his British mother, and knew then without a shadow of doubt that, hard as he found it to credit, this child *had* to be *his* son, *his* child, *his* responsibility. He moved away again, and Willow hovered, feeling entirely surplus to requirements, until one of the four bodyguards seated at a nearby table surged forward to pull out chairs at another table and Jai took a seat with Hari carefully cradled in his arms.

Willow dropped into the seat beside Jai's and Hari grinned at her while he tugged at Jai's tie. 'How did you find me?' she whispered.

'A private detective agency. They've been trying to trace you for months,' Jai imparted, his wide, sensual mouth compressing at that unfortunate fact. 'I only wish I'd found you sooner.'

'I can't imagine why you've been trying to find me,' she confided.

'But isn't it fortunate that I did?' Jai traded smoothly as he stroked a gentle finger through the spill of Hari's black hair. 'You must realise that you cannot stay in such a place with my son.'

Paper pale at that quiet declaration, Willow gazed back at him. '*Your*...son?' she almost whispered, shaken by the certainty with which he made that claim.

'He is my image. Who else's son could he be?' Jai parried very drily as if daring her to disagree or throw doubt on the question of his child's parentage. 'And as this is not somewhere that we can talk freely, I would like you to go back to your room right now and pack up all your belongings to leave.'

'I can't do that. I'm here waiting to get a place on

a council housing list and if I leave, I'll lose my place in the queue,' she protested in a low intent voice.

Jai settled Hari more securely on his lap. 'Either you do as I ask…*or* I will seek an emergency court order to take immediate custody of Hari as he is at risk in such an environment. That is unacceptable. Be warned that I hold diplomatic status in the UK and the authorities will act quickly on my behalf if I lodge a complaint on behalf of my heir. The usual laws do not apply to diplomats.'

In sheer shock at that menacing information, Willow went rigid, her blood chilling in her veins. 'You're threatening me with…legal action?' she gasped in astonishment, barely able to believe her ears. *'Already?'*

Jai sent her an inhumanly cool and calm appraisal, the dark strength of his resolve palpable. 'I will do what I must to put right what you have got wrong…'

Stabbed to the heart by that spontaneously of-fered opinion, Willow bent her head. *No judgement here*, she thought sarcastically, but she was so deep in shock that Jai would actually threaten her with losing custody of her child that she didn't even know what to say back to him. She didn't want to take the risk of being too frank, didn't want to row in public, didn't want to make a bad situation worse by speaking without careful forethought. She sensed that the

Jai she had thought she knew to some degree was not the Jai she was currently dealing with. This was Jai being ruthless and calculating and brutally confrontational, which, logic warned her, had to be qualities he had acquired to rise so high and so fast in the business world. Unluckily for her, it was not a side of him she had seen before or had had to deal with.

'We will not argue here in a public place,' Jai informed her in the same very polite tone. 'We will both ensure that the needs of our child remain our first consideration.'

'Of course, but—'

'No, there will be no qualification of that statement,' Jai interposed levelly. 'Now, please pack so that we can leave this place behind us.'

Willow leapt upright and reached down for Hari.

'I will look after him while you pack,' Jai spelt out as he too stood up, towering over her in her flat heels with Hari still clasped in his arms.

'You could walk away with him while I'm upstairs,' Willow pointed out shakily, not an ounce of colour in her taut face as she looked up at him fearfully.

'I give you my word of honour that I will not do that. You are his mother and my son needs his mother,' Jai murmured soft and low, the hardness of his expression softening a little. 'Although I grew up without mine, it would never be my choice to put my son in the same position.'

Willow backed off a step, still uncertain of what she should do. 'If I pack, where are you taking us to? A hotel?'

'Of course not. To my home here in London,' Jai proffered as Hari tugged cheerfully at his hair. 'I have already had rooms prepared for your arrival.'

'You took a lot for granted,' Willow remarked helplessly.

'In this situation, I can afford to do so,' Jai told her without remorse.

And with that ringing indictment of her ability to raise their child alone, Willow headed upstairs. There wasn't much for her to pack. She gathered up Hari's bottles and solid food and put them into the baby bag Shelley had bought her. She settled the bin bags filled with their clothing and Hari's toys into the battered stroller, donned her duffle coat and wheeled the stroller to the top of the stairs before stooping to lift it and battle to carry it downstairs. Halfway down the second flight one of Jai's bodyguards met her and lifted it out of her arms.

'Is that the lot?' Jai asked, turning from the reception desk, Hari tucked comfortably under one arm.

'Yes. I left stuff with Shelley.'

'There's a form for you to fill in. I put in the for-warding address,' Jai advanced.

Willow was surprised that there was only one form because before she had even moved into the hostel, she'd had to fill out a thirty-page document. She signed her name at the foot, briefly scanning the address Jai had filled in, raising a brow at the exclu-sivity of the area. Mayfair, no less. Five minutes later, she was climbing into a limousine for the first time in her life, breathless at the unknown ahead of her.

Jai strapped Hari into the car seat awaiting him.

'When did you learn to be so comfortable around babies?' Willow asked tautly.

'There are many children in my extended family. High days and holidays, they visit,' Jai told her. 'I was a lonely only child. Hari will never suffer from a lack of company.'

On her smoothly upholstered leather seat, Willow tensed, registering that Jai was already talking about her son visiting India. She supposed that was natural, and an expectation he would obviously have. Even so the prospect of her baby boy being so far away from her totally unnerved her, and she couldn't help feeling overwhelmed, most especially when Jai had already threatened her with legal action.

'Now for the question that taxes my patience the most,' Jai breathed, his nostrils flaring with annoyance, his light eyes throwing a laser-bright challenge. 'Why would you move into a homeless shelter rather than ask me for help?'

Willow froze. 'There's nothing wrong with living in a homeless shelter. They're there for when people are desperate.'

'But you weren't desperate, not really. You could've turned to me at any time. And don't try to misinterpret my question. I probably know a great deal more than you about the individuals who use such shelters. Some are those who have fallen on hard times through no fault of their own, others have mental health issues or are drug addicts or ex-cons. None of those elements make a homeless shelter safe or acceptable for a child,' Jai completed harshly.

'Nonetheless there are quite a few children living in them!' Willow shot back at him stubbornly.

'Why didn't you contact me?' Jai demanded, out of all patience with her reluctance to answer his original question. He had been denied all knowledge of his son for more than six months and that enraged him, but he was grimly aware that this was not the right time to reveal his deep anger, particularly not if he wanted her to tell him the truth.

Willow swallowed convulsively. 'I didn't think you'd want to know. It was my problem. He's my child.' She hesitated. 'When I was pregnant, I was afraid that you would want me to have a termination and I didn't want to be put in that position. I didn't want to feel guilty for wanting to have my own child. It was easier to get on with it on my own and I managed fine while I was pregnant and still able to work.'

'I would never have asked you to have a termination. Hari is my child too,' Jai retorted crisply. 'I would have ensured that you had somewhere decent to live and I would have supported you.'

Willow sighed. 'Well, it's too late now to be arguing about it.'

Jai's eyes flashed at that assurance and he struggled to repress his anger, because her misplaced pride and lack of faith in him had ensured that his son had endured living conditions that were far less than his due.

'So, how *did* you manage to conceive when you told me it would be safe for us to have sex?' he asked next, battening down his volatile responses to concentrate on the basic facts.

Willow could feel her whole face heating up and she glanced across at Jai with noticeable reluctance. *Safe* to have sex? That was what he had meant that night? She shook her head slowly as clarity spilled through her brain and she squirmed in retrospect over her own stupidity. 'I misunderstood. When you asked if it was safe, I assumed that you were asking if we would be interrupted…if I was expecting any-one,' she admitted stiffly, her cheeks only burning more fierily at the look of incredulity that flared in his ice-blue eyes. 'I'm sorry. I wasn't thinking about contraception. That danger honestly didn't cross my mind.'

And the whole mystery of how she had become pregnant was clarified there and then, Jai conceded in a kind of wonderment. She had misunderstood him, and he had been too hot for her to reflect on the risk that he had never taken with any other woman. They had had unprotected sex several times because the young woman he had slept with had still had the mentality of a guilty, self-conscious teenager, deter-mined to hide her sex life from the critical grown-ups. He supposed then that he had got exactly what he deserved for not considering questioning the level of her sexual experience.

Or was he being very naive in accepting that ex-planation? Was it, indeed, possible that Willow had *wanted* to become pregnant by a rich man? A rich man and a baby by him could secure a woman's com-fort for a comfortable twenty years. In one calculat-ing move, such a pregnancy would have solved all Willow's financial problems. And not contacting him and keeping him out of the picture until the child was safely born could well have been part of the same gold-digging scheme to set him up and profit from her fertility in the future.

Jai frowned, ice-blue eyes, enhanced by velvety black lashes, turning glacier cool as he surveyed her. She looked tired and tense and hadn't made any effort to do herself up for his benefit, but then, why would she bother when she was now the mother of his son and already in an unassailable position in his life?

At the same time, he had made the first move that night after the funeral, at least, he *thought* he had. In truth, all he recalled was the heady taste of her lips, not *how* he had arrived at that point. The pulse at his groin kicked up a storm at that recollection, reminding him that he was still hungry for her. His jaw clenched. He would soon find out if she was mercenary and, really, it didn't matter a damn, did it? After all, whatever she was, whoever she turned out to be, he *had* to marry her for his son's sake…

CHAPTER FOUR

WILLOW WALKED INTO the Mayfair town house and was plunged straight into palatial contemporary décor that was breathtakingly large and impressive.

'Come this way,' Jai instructed, heading straight for the elegant staircase with Hari still clasped to his powerful chest. 'My former *ayah*, Shanaya, arrived this morning. She has a full complement of staff with her and they will look after Hari while we talk.'

'Ayah?' Willow questioned with frowning eyes.

'She was my nursemaid…nanny—whatever you want to call it,' Jai explained. 'She is a kind and gentle woman. You need have no fear for our son's welfare while he is with her.'

Willow didn't want to hand over care of Hari to anyone, no matter who they were, particularly when she could not imagine that she and Jai had much to discuss. He had threatened her to make her vacate the homeless shelter and he doubtless planned to press his advantage by making her accept his financial support. Using the threat of legal action straight away had warned her that he would not listen to her protests. His bottom line, his closing argument would always zero in on what was best for Hari. And how could she argue with that sterling rule when she wanted the same thing?

Therefore, bearing in mind that she did not expect to be spending very long in Jai's luxurious town house, she pinned a pleasant smile to her face to greet the grey-haired older woman awaiting her in a room already furnished as a nursery. She had three smiling younger women by her side, all of them dressed in brightly coloured saris, and they welcomed Hari with a sort of awed reverence that disconcerted Willow. Hari, however, did love to be admired and he beamed at all of them.

'His Royal Highness is very confident,' Shanaya remarked approvingly in hesitant English.

'His Royal Highness?' Willow hissed in disbelief as Jai whisked her back out of the room again.

'Hari is my official heir, known as the Yuvaraja in our language. He is a very important child to my family and to our staff,' Jai explained, ushering her downstairs and into a very traditional library lined with books and pictures and what looked like a wall of official awards. 'This was my father's room and, although I have certainly not kept it like a shrine, I did not have it updated after his death like the rest of the house. I still like to remember him seated here at his desk or drowsing by the fireside with his nose in a book.'

Willow had faded memories of the older man on his visits to the boarding school, which he had once attended himself. She also recalled him taking tea once in their small home with her father, the correctness of his spoken English, the warmth of his smile and the tiny brocade box filled with sweets that he had dug out of his pocket for her.

'It means a great deal to me that you named our son after me,' Jai admitted.

Willow went pink. 'I wanted to acknowledge his background.'

'Hari has been a family name for generations. My father would have rejoiced in our son's existence.'

'In these circumstances?' Willow said uncomfortably. 'I hardly think so.'

'I assume you are referring to Hari's illegitimate birth,' Jai breathed in a raw undertone. 'That problem will vanish as soon as we marry.'

Willow's knees shook under her and she had to straighten her back to stay upright. Her incredulous gaze locked to his lean, dark features and the flaring brilliance of his pale gaze. 'I beg your pardon?' she murmured with a frown. 'As soon as we...*marry*?'

'Hari's birth will be legitimised by our marriage. He cannot take his place as my heir *without* us getting married,' Jai countered levelly. 'I want us to get married as quickly as it can be arranged.'

Willow gave up the battle with her wobbly knees and dropped heavily into a comfortable armchair beside the Georgian fireplace. Slowly she shook her head. 'Jai...men and women don't get married any more simply because a child has been born.'

'Perhaps not, but Hari can only claim his legal right to follow me if we are man and wife. It may seem old-fashioned to you, but it is the law and it is unlikely to be changed. My inheritance, which will one day become his, is safeguarded by strict rules. My business interests I can leave to anyone I want, but my heritage, the properties and land involved and the charitable foundation started up by my grandfather can only be bestowed on the firstborn child, whose parents must be married for him to inherit,' Jai outlined grimly.

Disconcerted by that information, Willow snatched in a deep jagged breath. 'But you can't *want* to marry me?'

'I don't want to marry anyone right now,' Jai admitted wryly.

Willow stiffened, reckoning that she had just received her answer about how best to treat his prop-
osition. His suggestion that they should marry was
sheer madness, she reasoned in astonishment. Her
entire attention was now welded to him. A blue-
black shadow of stubble was beginning to accen-
tuate his wide mobile mouth and a tiny little shiver
ran through her, her breasts tightening and peaking
below her sweater, those little sensations arrowing
down into her pelvis to awaken a hot, tense, damp
feeling between her thighs. She thrust her spine rig-
idly into the embrace of the chair back, furious with
herself but breathless and unable to drag her attention from the wild dark beauty of Jai as he paced
over to the desk, his stunning eyes glittering over
her with an intensity she could *feel* and which mesmerised her.

'Obviously you don't *want* to marry me,' she remarked in a brittle undertone.

'Aside of my little flirtation with the idea of marriage when I was twenty-one, I have always hoped to
retain my freedom for as long as possible,' Jai confessed with a twist of his shapely mouth as he studied her, appreciating the elegant delicacy of her tiny
figure in the overly large chair, but not appreciating
the way his attention instinctively lingered on the
swell of her breasts below the sweater and the slen-

der stretch of her denim-clad thighs. 'I planned to marry in my forties, while my father was even older when he took the plunge. Hari's birth, however, has changed everything. I cannot deny Hari his right to enjoy the same history and privileges that I had.'

'I understand that, *but*—' she began emotively.

'No matter what you say, it will still come down to the same conclusion. Our son *needs* his parents to be married,' Jai delivered with biting finality. 'Only imagine his angry bitterness if some day he has to watch another man inherit what should have been his…because *if* you refuse to marry me, I will inevitably marry another woman and have children with her. It is my duty to carry on our family name and a second son born from that marriage will become my heir instead.'

The content of that last little speech shook Willow rigid because she realised that she didn't want to imagine *any* of those events taking place…*not* Jai marrying someone else and fathering children by her and certainly *not* her son hurt by being nudged out of what could have been his rightful place. It was a distressing picture, but Jai was being realistic when he forced her to look at it. Sooner or later, it seemed, he had to marry and have a child and why shouldn't his firstborn son benefit from their marriage?

'You're ready to bite the bullet because Hari and

I would be the practical option?' Willow suggested tightly.

'Those are not the words I would have used,' Jai chided. 'This may not be what I once innocently planned, but Hari is here now and, as his parents, shouldn't we do what we can to make amends for his current status?'

Willow stared stonily at the rug on the floor, because it was an unanswerable question. Of course, Hari should be put first, not left to reap the disadvantages his careless parents had left him facing. Would her son even want to follow in his father's footsteps to eventually become the Maharaja of Chandrapur? She reckoned that, as an adult, her son would want that choice and wouldn't wish to be denied it over something as arbitrary as the accident of his birth. She swallowed hard. 'Right, so if I agree to marry you, what sort of marriage would it be?'

'A normal one,' Jai murmured, soft and low, a little of his tension dissipating as he grasped that she was willing to proceed. 'Of course, if we are unhappy together we can separate and divorce but we will both make a big effort for Hari's sake because two parents raising him together must surely be better than only one.'

Of course, neither of them knew what it would be like to grow up with two parents, Willow conceded.

But she had seen that dynamic in the homes of her friends, parents pulling and working together to look after their families. She had also visited the homes of single-parent families and had only noted there that the parent carried a much heavier burden in doing it all alone. Would she and Jai be able to provide Hari with a secure and happy home? Jai didn't love her, while she was still insanely attracted to him, she acknowledged uneasily, lifting her head to collide with the frosty glitter of his eyes, feeling the almost painful clench of internal muscles deep down inside.

'Do you think we could do it?' she whispered.

'I think we *must* for his benefit,' Jai countered levelly. 'And as soon as possible. Are we agreed?'

Almost mesmerised by the blaze of his full attention, Willow nodded very slowly. 'Yes.'

She was going to marry Jai and the concept was surreal: Jai the playboy with his polo ponies and trophies, his heritage palaces, his long backstory of glamorous and impossibly beautiful former lovers. Yet she was so ordinary, so unexciting in comparison, she thought in dismay. Even worse, he didn't want to marry *her* and he had admitted it.

But that honesty of his was good, she told herself fiercely. Should she be ashamed of the reality that the very idea of being freed from all her financial worries was a relief? Did that mean that she was greedy? Or simply that she was tired of feeling like an inadequate mother? Without Jai, she had found it impossible to give Hari the comfort and security he deserved. With Jai, everything would be different. In addition, she would have far more rights over her own son if she married Jai. In terms of custody they would be equal partners then, she reasoned, and no matter what happened between her and Jai she would have very little reason to fear losing access to her little boy.

What would it be like, though, being married to a man who didn't love or really want her? Jai hadn't even wanted her enough to ask to *see* her again, she reminded herself doggedly, reeling from the toxic bite of that fact. Yes, sure, he had tried to check up on her a couple of months afterwards, she conceded grudgingly, but by that stage only an ingrained sense of responsibility towards Brian Allerton's daughter had been driving him, nothing more personal.

Of course, she didn't love him either, she reminded herself doggedly. All the same, she couldn't take her eyes off Jai when he was in the same room and her heart hammered and her mouth ran dry every time he looked at her. If she was honest with herself, she was sort of fascinated by Jai, always hungry to know more about him and work out what made

him tick. He had accepted Hari without question and
moved them straight into his home.

Yes, he had threatened her with legal action but
only on Hari's behalf, not to take her son away
from her, indeed only, it seemed, to pressure her
into leaving the hostel and agreeing to marry him.
With shocking shrewdness, he had accomplished
that objective within hours, she registered in belated
dismay. Yet he had done it even though at heart he
didn't *want* to marry her! But that was the mystery
that was Jai. He was volatile and emotional and very
hot-blooded, yet he was still apparently willing to
settle for a practical marriage…

Jai watched Willow walk away from him to return
to their son. Evidently, he was about to acquire a
wife. He gritted his teeth, for being forced to marry
to bring Hari officially into the family was even less
attractive than increasing age prompting him to the
challenge. Marriage was difficult, as his parents'
failure to surmount their differences proved. But he
knew in his heart that he *owed* Willow a wedding
ring. It *was* that simple, because what he had done
with her broke every principle he had been raised to
respect: he had greedily and irresponsibly taken an
innocent woman and slept with her when she was

vulnerable, and even in the act he had not protected her as he should've done.

He found it hard, though, to forgive her for hiding Hari from him and denying him precious moments of his son's babyhood that would never be repeated. But he had to set that anger aside, he reminded himself fiercely, shelve the pointless regrets that he could have been such an idiot and concentrate instead on the present. He should be relieved that she still attracted him, even if he resented the constant disturbing pull of her understated sensuality. He didn't know how she still had that effect on him, and he wasn't planning to explore it again, not until they were safely, decently married.

'You look a treat,' Shelley said, patting Willow's hand as they travelled in a limousine to the civil ceremony at the register office.

Willow shivered, scolding herself for having picked a wedding dress unsuited to autumn, but then she had been living on a dizzy merry-go-round of change and struggling to adapt throughout the past week in Jai's London home. Agreeing to marry Jai had been like jumping on an express train that hurtled along at breakneck speed. He had pointed out that getting married in Chandrapur would entail a solid week of festivities while getting married *dis-*

creetly in London would only require an hour and a couple of witnesses.

She had spent most of the week with Hari because Jai had been busy working. She had, however, seen Jai at mealtimes and had tripped over him in the nursery more than once. Surrounded by a bevy of admiring nursemaids, Jai was attempting to get to know his son and Hari was thriving on the amount of attention he was receiving. Willow could already see that the biggest problem of her son's new lifestyle would be ensuring that Hari did not grow up into an over-indulged young man, unacquainted with the word 'no.'

Her wedding gown left her arms and throat bare. With cap sleeves, a crystal-beaded corset top and a sparkly tulle skirt, it was a fairy-tale dress and very bridal. In retrospect, Willow was embarrassed about the choice she had made and worried that it was too excessive for the occasion. But who knew if she would ever get married again? And when she was faced with choosing her one and possibly *only* wedding dress, she had gone with her heart.

Luckily, she had had Shelley's support when a stylist had arrived at the house and informed her that she had been instructed to provide Willow with a whole new wardrobe. A huge wardrobe of clothes tailored to fit Willow had been delivered within forty-eight hours, outfits chosen to shine at any possible occasion and many of the options decidedly grand. Hari now also rejoiced in many changes of exclusive baby clothing. Jai, Willow reckoned ruefully, was re-writing their history and redesigning his bride into a far more fashionable and exclusive version of herself. Did he appreciate that that determination to improve her appearance only revealed that he had previously found her unpolished and gauche?

She walked into the anteroom with Shelley by her side. Jai approached her with his best friend, Sher, and performed an introduction. Sher was the Nizam of Tharistan and he and Jai had been childhood play-mates. Sher was tall, black-haired and as sleekly handsome as a Bollywood movie star. Beside her, she felt Shelley breathe in deep and slow as though she was bracing herself and she almost laughed at her friend's susceptibility to a good-looking man until it occurred to her that she was even more sus-ceptible to Jai.

'You chose a beautiful dress,' Jai murmured. 'It will look most appropriate in the photographs.'

'What photographs?' she asked with a frown.

'I have organised a photographer to record the oc-casion. Brides and grooms always want to capture such precious memories on film, I believe,' he ad-vanced calmly. 'A photo will be released to the local media in Chandrapur and some day Hari may wish to look at them.'

Willow grasped that he had wanted her to look suitably bridal in the photographs and understood that there was nothing personal in the compliment. He was simply keen for her to visibly fit the bridal role so that the haste that had prompted their marriage was less obvious.

They entered the room where the ceremony was to take place. Willow focussed on a rather tired-looking display of flowers in a cheap vase and tensed as Jai threaded the wedding ring onto her finger. She turned in the circle of his arms, thinking numbly, *I am married to Jai now,* but it didn't feel remotely real. It felt like a fevered dream, much as that night in his arms had felt.

It felt a little more real when she shivered on the steps outside and posed for the photographer that awaited them. Jai smiled down at her, that killer smile of his that made her stupid heart flutter like a trapped bird inside her chest, and she remembered him smiling down at her that night in the aftermath of satisfaction. And, of course, Jai was pleased, she told herself ruefully—he had accomplished exactly what he wanted for Hari.

They returned to the house for a light lunch. Hari

was brought down to meet Sher and then Sher offered to give Shelley a lift home.

'Does he have a limousine?' Willow asked with amusement in her clear eyes after she had hugged her scatty friend and promised to invite her out to Chandrapur for her annual holiday.

'I should think so. Sher made his fortune in the film world before he went into business,' Jai told her. 'And we need to make tracks now for the airport.'

'I'll get changed.' But, still immobile, Willow hovered in the hall as Jai closed the distance between them and reached for her, his eyes as bright as a silvery blue polar flame.

'It is a shame that you have to take off that dress without me to do the honours,' Jai husked soft and low, his fiery attention locking so intently to the luscious pout of her pink lips that a convulsive shiver rippled through her slender frame. 'But if I joined you now, if I even dared to *touch* you, we would never make the flight this side of tomorrow.'

Her breath feathered dangerously in her throat, her entire body quickening and pulsing in response to that heated appraisal and the smooth eroticism of those words while he kept his lean, powerful frame carefully separate from hers. Her five senses were screaming with a hunger that hurt, the achingly familiar scent of him, which only made her want to be closer to taste him, the tingling in her fingertips at the prospect of touching him, the rasp of his dark deep voice in her ears throwing up the recollection of his ecstatic groan in the darkness of the night. It was an overwhelmingly potent combination.

'Go upstairs, *soniyaa*,' Jai urged thickly.

On trembling legs, Willow spun away, only to get a few steps and halt again to turn back to him. 'What does that mean?'

'In Hindi? Beautiful one,' he translated.

Shaken, Willow climbed the stairs, breathless from the spell he had cast over her, the sheer shocking effect of that high-voltage sexuality focussed on her again. And yet he had not touched her once since she had moved into his house, had left her alone in her bed, maintaining a polite and pleasant attitude without a hint of intimacy when they met at occasional mealtimes. Why was that? Why had he kept his distance even after she had agreed to marry him?

It had made Willow feel that his former attraction to her had been a short-lived thing, a flash in the pan, one of those weird, almost inexplicable incidents that struck only in a moment of temptation. Now it seemed that Jai was much more drawn to her than he had been willing to reveal but, while he had maintained his reserve, he had damaged her self-esteem because the awareness that she still craved him when he did not seem to return that compliment or share that weakness had felt humiliating.

After checking on Hari, who was enjoying a comfortable nap after his midday feed, Willow changed into one of her new outfits, an elegant fitted sheath dress and slender high heels teamed with a jacket for the cooler temperatures of London.

She had never travelled in a private jet before and Jai's was spectacularly well-appointed in terms of comfort and space. She sat down beside Hari's crib in the sleeping compartment and fell deeply, dreamlessly asleep. Jai glanced in at the two of them and when he saw her curled up on the bed next to his son's crib, his chest tightened, and he breathed in deep and slow. They were his wife and child, his family now, and, in spite of what he had expected, he didn't feel trapped. No, so intense was his hunger for her that he couldn't think further than the night ahead when that raw hunger would finally be sated.

Willow's strawberry-blond waves tumbled across the pristine pillow, her soft mouth tranquil, her heart-shaped face relaxed in slumber. She was a beauty and his tribe of relatives would greet her like manna from heaven for they had long awaited his marriage. Hari would simply be the cherry on the top of an award-winning cake.

Willow wakened to the news that they were landing at Chandrapur in half an hour and with the time difference it was almost lunchtime. Hari occupied the first fifteen minutes until Shanaya took over and the remainder of the time Willow hurtled around showering and changing.

Jai's bodyguards moved round them as their party emerged from the VIP channel and a roar of sound met her ears. Dozens of photographers were leaning over the barriers with cameras and shouting questions. The flashes blinded her. Until that unsettling moment she had forgotten how famous Jai was in his birth country. Single as well as very good-looking and immensely successful, he was highly photogenic and a media dream. His sports exploits on the polo field, his business achievements and the gloss of his playboy lifestyle provided plenty of useful gossip-column fodder.

'Sorry about that. I should've timed the announcement of our marriage better,' Jai breathed above her head as he steered her down a quiet corridor and back out to the sunlit tarmac. The heat of midday was more than she had expected as she scanned the clear blue sky above them and she was relieved to climb into the waiting vehicle that, Jai assured her, would quickly whisk them to journey's end.

'Where's Hari?' she gasped worriedly.

'In the car behind us. I often make this transfer

by helicopter but Shanaya doesn't trust a helicopter
with a child as precious as Hari.' Jai chuckled.

Precious, Willow savoured, enjoying that word
being linked to her son. A crush of noisy traffic surrounded them, and she peered out of the windows.
There were a lot of trucks and cars, colourful tuk-
tuks painted with bright advertisements and many
motorbikes with women in bright saris riding side-
saddle behind the driver in what looked like a very
precarious position. Horns blared, vehicles moved
off and then ground to a sudden halt again to allow
a herd of sacred bulls to wander placidly through
the traffic. Bursts of loud music filtered into the car
as they drove along beside a lake. By the side of the
dusty road she saw dancers gyrating.

'It's a festival day and the streets are crammed.
Luckily our palace isn't far,' Jai remarked.

Our palace.

Willow almost smiled at the designation, for she
had never dreamt that those two words used together
would ever feature in her future. 'So, you're taking
me to where your family's story began—'

'No. My family's story began at the fortress in
the fourteenth century. Look out of the window,' Jai
urged. 'See the fort on the crags above the city…'

Willow looked up in wonder at the vast red sandstone fortress sprawling across the cliffs above the

city. 'My ancestor first invaded Chandrapur in the thirteenth century. It took his family a hundred and forty years of assaults and sieges but eventually they conquered the fort. We will visit it next week,' he promised. 'At present it's full of tourists…we would have no privacy.'

'Then, where are we going now?'

'The Lake Palace,' Jai told her lazily. 'It's surrounded by water and a private wildlife reserve and immensely private. It is where I make my home.'

'So you like…have a *choice* of palaces to use?' Willow was gobsmacked by the concept of having a selection.

'The third one is half palace, half hotel, built by my great-grandfather in high deco style in the twenties. We will visit there too,' Jai assured her calmly.

'*Three?* And that's it…here?' Willow checked.

'There is also the Monsoon Palace. A very much loved and spoilt wife in the sixteenth century accounts for that one,' Jai proffered almost apologetically. 'I leave it to the tourists.'

'You own an awful lot of property,' Willow remarked numbly.

'And now you own it too…as Sher reminded me, I didn't ask you to sign a pre-nuptial agreement,' Jai parried, shocking and startling her with that comment.

'We did get married in a hurry,' Willow conceded ruefully.

'Let us hope that neither of us live to regret that omission,' Jai murmured without expression.

'I'm not greedy. If we ever split up,' Willow told him in a rush, rising above the sinking sensation in her stomach at that concept, 'I won't *ever* try to take what's not mine. I'm very conscious that I entered this marriage with nothing and all I would ask for is enough to keep Hari and I somewhere secure and comfortable.'

'My biggest fear would be losing daily access to my son,' Jai confided with a harsh edge to his dark, deep voice.

Willow suppressed a shiver. 'Let's not even talk about it,' she muttered, turning to look at a quartet of women, their beautiful veils floating in the breeze as they carried giant metal water containers on their heads.

On both sides of the road stretched the desert, where only groves of acacia bushes, milk thistle and spiky grass grew in the sand. It was a hard, unforgiving land where water was of vital importance and only a couple of miles further on, where irrigation had been made possible, lay an oasis of small fields of crops and greenery, which utterly transformed the landscape.

His hand covered her tense fingers. 'We won't let anything split us up,' Jai told her. 'Hari's happiness depends on us staying together.'

'Did you miss your mother so much?' Willow heard herself ask without even thinking.

'I was a baby when she deserted my father and I have no memory of her,' Jai admitted flatly as he removed his hand from hers. 'I met her only once as an adult. I don't talk about my mother...*ever*.'

Willow swallowed painfully hard as her cheeks burned in receipt of that snub and she knew that she wouldn't be raising that thorny topic again.

CHAPTER FIVE

THEY DROVE ALONG a heavily wooded and fenced road and over a very decorative bridge on which a cluster of pale grey monkeys was perched. A tall archway ushered the car into a large central courtyard, ringed by a vast two-storey white building, picturesquely ornamented with domed roofs and a pillared frontage. Only then did Willow appreciate that they had arrived at the Lake Palace.

As she climbed out of the car, she was surprised to see a group of colourfully clad musicians drumming and playing with enthusiasm to greet their arrival. A trio of maids hurried down the steps fronting the long pillared façade of the building, bearing cool drinks, hot cloths for freshening up and garlands of marigolds. Behind them, from every corner of the complex poured more staff.

'It's traditional,' Jai dismissed when she gaped and commented.

'But why on earth do you employ so many people?'

Jai frowned. 'My father raised me to believe that our role in society is to provide employment wherever we can. Yes, I appreciate that we don't *need* the five-star triumphal welcome that my ancestors all enjoyed, but you must also appreciate that those who serve us rely on their employment here. One person may be responsible for keeping an entire tribe of relatives. Never seek to cut household costs unless you see evidence of dishonesty,' he warned her.

'I wasn't criticising,' Willow backtracked uncomfortably, self-consciously skimming her gaze across the lush garden fronting the palace instead. Glorious shrubs were in full bloom all around them. She couldn't immediately identify even one of the shrubs and was immediately keen to explore a new world of tropical plants. She turned as the other cars drew up behind them and immediately moved forward to reclaim Hari from Shanaya, her heart lifting as her son greeted her with a huge smile.

'I keep up the traditions as my father did,' Jai murmured softly by her side, lifting his son from her as the baby stretched out a hand to touch him and screwed up his face at his failure to make contact with his father. 'I employ as many people as possible. When I was younger, I was less far-seeing. When a household custom seemed outdated, I banned it, but it wasn't always possible for those involved to find another position on my staff. Modernising is to be welcomed but not if it means I'm putting people on the breadline to achieve it.'

'I understand,' Willow murmured, aware of the stares from the assembled staff, whom Jai invited closer to see their son. The level of their appreciation for the little boy in Jai's arms warmed her from inside out.

One of the gardeners approached her with a beautiful pink and yellow flower and extended it to her before bowing very low.

'He is proud to be the first to welcome the new Maharani to her home and he swears that even the frangipani blossom is not your equal,' Jai translated with an amused grin.

They walked into a huge circular hall fashioned entirely of marble and supported on carved pillars while Jai directed her towards the curving staircase and up to the landing. He walked down an imposing corridor lined with portraits of the former Maharajas of Chandrapur and showed her into a room already set up as a nursery for Hari.

Willow reclaimed her son and sat down with him.

'When you're free I'll join you for a late lunch. I have some work matters to take care of,' Jai told her before leaving again.

Hari needed to be changed and fed and there were innumerable staff hovering, eager to take care of his needs for her, but Willow didn't want to lose her position of being first and foremost in her baby's life, nor did she want him exposed to too many new faces and different childcare practices at once. Overpowered by the grandeur of Jai's home, she also needed a moment or two of doing ordinary things to feel comfortable again. Thanking everyone cheerfully for the help she wouldn't accept, she saw to Hari herself before finally laying him down for his nap.

When she emerged from the nursery again, a moustachioed man in a bright red turban and traditional attire spread open an inlaid brass door on the other side of the landing and bowed his head in a deferential invitation. Willow passed by him into the most breathtaking interior and her steps slowed as she paused to admire the intricate glass mosaic tiles set into the walls to make superb pictures of a bygone age. Depicted on the walls were hunting scenes with elephants and tigers and grand and very vivid ceremonial processions. Talking on his phone, Jai was striding across the shaded terrace beyond the room that overlooked the lake. In that airy space a table and chairs were arranged.

Willow watched him move, absorbing the elegant grace of his lean, powerful figure as he moved and talked, spreading expressive fingers, shifting his hands this way and that in fluid stress or dismissal of a point. A thrill of desire pierced her soft and deep, making her breath catch in her throat. He was so extremely good-looking and she was married to him now, which still didn't seem real to her. His head turned as he noticed her hovering for the first time and the heat of his stare sent the blood drumming up beneath her skin.

Willow sank down into a dining chair. A napkin was laid over her lap with a flourish by a bearded middle-aged man.

'This is Ranjit,' Jai explained, dropping his phone down on the tabletop and settling down opposite her. 'He speaks excellent English and oversees our household. Anything you need, you ask him, and he will provide it. After we've eaten, I'll show you around.'

'It's a fascinating building and the surroundings only make it more exotic,' she commented, watching a crocodile slide off a mudflat into the lake, his two beady eyes creepy bumps above the surface as he swam. 'But I shouldn't like to meet that gator on a dark night.'

'For safety we only ever leave this building in vehicles. I'll take you on a mini safari some afternoon, although it's amazing how many of the animals you can view from up here. Sooner or later, they all visit the water. He's not a gator, by the way, he's a marsh crocodile.'

'I don't know much about wild animals,' she confided. 'Only what I've learned from watching documentaries. Tell me, why so many palaces?'

'Every generation wanted to be current. Centuries ago this palace and the land around it was for the royal family to hunt.' Jai grimaced. 'And now it's a wildlife reserve. The original fortress above the city is magnificent but could not possibly be adapted to modern life and my grandfather's deco palace is more of a showpiece than a home. Approximately two thirds of that building is now an award-winning hotel and the remaining wing remains ours. We will entertain my relatives and friends there at a party to be held in a few weeks to celebrate our marriage. Is there anyone you wish to invite on your own behalf?'

'No relatives left alive,' she reminded him. 'And no friends who could afford to fly out to India just for a party.'

'I would cover the expense for any of your guests. Shelley?'

Willow winced and coloured. 'She has no holiday leave left. She had to take time off to help me with Hari after he was born.'

His ebony brows furrowed. 'Why? Was he very challenging?'

'No, I was the problem,' Willow confessed. 'I had to have an emergency Caesarean and it was a couple of weeks before I was fit enough to look after him on my own. They don't keep you in hospital after surgery for long these days.'

Jai compressed his lips. 'And yet you *still* didn't think of contacting me for help?'

'We got through it,' Willow muttered with a troubled shrug.

'Why…an emergency?' he pressed. 'What happened?'

'I'd been in labour for hours and it wasn't progressing as it should've done. Hari was a big baby and they had to operate for his sake.' Willow relaxed a little as the food arrived and relaxed even more when she registered that it was entirely a British chicken meal without even a hint of spice.

Jai's high cheekbones were prominent beneath his bronzed skin. He could have lost his son without ever knowing he existed. He could have lost Willow as well. The acknowledgement shook him and her lack of guilt on that score annoyed him, no matter how hard he worked at suppressing such negative reactions. Jai was accustomed to being in charge, used to women who were eager to please him, certainly not a woman who shunned his support and thrust her independence unapologetically in his face. Or perhaps it was the fact that she *still* refused to admit that she had made a mistake in not telling him that she was pregnant. Had behaved as though he could have no possible importance as a father in his son's life.

Or, more probably, had she thought of her own father's cruel indifference to her feelings when she'd failed to meet his exacting academic standards? Possibly she had decided that a father figure was not so necessary. Jai, however, had enjoyed a father who was caring and supportive and it was a role he took very seriously. Suddenly impatient, he thrust his plate away and stood up.

'Let me show you the palace,' he urged, watching as she rose to her feet, her jewelled eyes bright in her heart-shaped face, her lush mouth pink and succulent. Even as he dragged his attention from her mouth, he was hard and full and throbbing. The result of more than a year's celibacy, he told himself in exasperation. In those circumstances, it was natural, even normal, for him to be almost embarrassingly wound up. He had not gone that long without sex since he became an adult. There was no reason whatsoever for him to get worked up about the prospect of having sex with his wife when it was a purely practical element of a marriage undertaken simply to confirm his son's status.

He escorted her downstairs to the two-storey library that had been his father's pride and joy. Sheltered beneath one of the domes, it rejoiced in a twisting narrow marble staircase to the upper floor.

Willow stopped dead to look around herself in amazement at the towering columns of bookcases. In several places there were alcoves backed by stained-glass window embrasures and upholstered with comfortable cushions, little reading nooks, she registered in fascination, never having entered so inviting a library space. 'It's absolutely gorgeous,' she murmured appreciatively. 'I may not be academic but I love to read, so it's ironic that all the books here will mostly be in another language.'

'No. There are many English books in this library.' Jai watched her sink down into one of the reading nooks. A tiny delicate figure in a pale blue dress that somehow brought out the peach glints in her hair and the perfect clarity of her porcelain skin, against which her green eyes gleamed like emeralds.

Willow inched back on her elbows until she was fully reclined, her head resting back against a soft cushion, and grinned. 'I can tell you now… I'll be spending time in here.'

Jai studied her with helpless intensity. She was entirely unaware of her own appeal, entirely divorced from the reality that her hem had ridden up and a deeply erotic view of the space between her slender thighs was open to him. Without even being aware of it, prompted more by his senses than by anything else, Jai moved closer. 'You're the most beautiful thing in here,' he said in a driven undertone.

'Less of the sauce, Jai…as Shelley would say,' Willow teased, coming up on her elbows again and preparing to get up. 'I'm not and have never been a beauty. You don't need to say that sort of stuff to me just because we're married. I don't expect it.'

Jai moved so fast she was startled when he came down over her, caging her in the nook with his lean, powerful body. 'I very rarely say anything I don't mean,' he rasped, coming down to her to claim her mouth with a hungry brevity that only made her crave him more. 'It is for me to tell you that you are beautiful, not for you to disagree, because what would *you* know about it?'

Willow blinked, disconcerted by that sudden kiss. 'Well…er…'

'Because you haven't got a clue!' Jai growled in reproof, pushing down on her with his lean hips and shifting with sinuous grace against her pelvis to acquaint her with his arousal.

It was the most primal thing he had ever done to her and it set Willow on fire, inside and out. It was as though he'd lit a pulse in the most sensitive area of her body, a part of herself she had more or less forgotten existed after the discovery that she was pregnant. There had been no more lying awake restless in the night hours, shifting in frustration while she wantonly recalled the heated expertise of his body on hers. No, she had shut that sensual side down, recognising that that was what had got her into trouble in the first instance and that, with a child on the way, she had more important stuff to focus on. But in that moment, there was *nothing* more important than the powerful allure of Jai's hot-blooded invitation and the wanting took her by storm. Her arms reached up of their own seeming volition and snaked round his neck to pull him down to her.

'No, *not* here…perhaps some other day but not on what is virtually our wedding night,' Jai specified authoritatively.

Willow pushed him back from her, the taste of humiliation burning in her cheeks and souring in her mouth, which had so readily, so eagerly opened for his. She came upright, smoothing down her rucked-up frock like a bristling kitten. He was always so much in control that it infuriated her at that moment. One minute he was luring her in, the next pushing her away! It bore too many reminders of how much he had craved her that first night in contrast with his cold withdrawal the next morning.

'One of the servants is sweeping rugs on the upper

level,' Jai added in an undertone. 'I could order him to leave but it seems unnecessary when we have a bedroom.'

'I suppose by the time you get to your age you get settled in your ways!' Willow snapped back at him tartly, because she was mortified and not really listening, had been so far gone to common sense indeed for several seconds as she reached for him that she wouldn't have noticed if a trumpet band had marched past her. 'I'm more of an al fresco kind of girl!' she added, even though she wasn't quite sure that those two words matched what she had intended to convey: an image of her being more sexually brave and adventurous than he was, which was of course ridiculous when he was the only man she had ever been with and his experience was presumably much greater than hers.

'No. I know that my bride deserves a level of care and esteem from me that she did not receive on the last occasion we were together,' Jai countered flatly, wondering what other sexual expectations she had of him, coming to grips with that apparent challenge with a shot of adrenalin charging through his veins.

In reality, Jai had never been challenged or questioned in the bedroom. Women invariably reacted as though everything he did there was incredible and told him so repeatedly. For the first time he wondered if it was a fact that he *was* too conservative, raised as he had been by a rather elderly parent from a different generation from those of his peers, a father with a distinctly Victorian take on the opposite sex.

Willow rolled her eyes at him, eyes that turned a darker catlike green in temper, he noted, marvelling that he had gone twenty-nine years on Planet Earth without ever before meeting a woman prepared to disagree with him. On the surface she seemed so mild in temperament and shy, although she was a wild woman in bed, Jai acknowledged, reaching for her hand, finding she snatched her fingers back, smiling because he was genuinely amused.

. And that sunlit smile of Jai's steamrollered the temper out of Willow as though he had thrown a bucket of water over her because, deep down inside, she *knew* she was being childish, bitter and insecure and that he hadn't earned that response. She looked up at him and those eyes of his were bright between lush black curling lashes and her heart literally went ka-boom inside her and clenched. She slid her hand back into his and in silence they left the library.

'I'll show you the rest of the place some other time,' Jai told her, walking her along the corridor to the double doors at the other end of the landing. A servant somehow contrived to snake at phenomenal speed round from the other side of the landing and throw the doors open for them and quietly shut them again in their wake.

The main bedroom was another awe-inspiring room, all of a glitter, with flowers and foliage hand-painted in shades of cream and gold with tiny inset mirrors everywhere on the walls, reflecting light into an interior that could otherwise have seemed dark because there were no windows. Instead there were densely carved stone screens open to the elements to filter in fresh air.

'It was remodelled a century ago. It used to be part of the *zenana* where the royal women lived in *purdah*, only allowed to be seen by male family members. My father could still remember elderly relatives who grew up in that lifestyle, men and women living separately,' Jai told her softly as she fingered the screen to look out through the tiny holes to the courtyard below, trying to imagine what it would have been like to only have a view of a life one was not allowed to actively share.

'It must've been horrible,' she whispered, her tiny nose wrinkling up expressively.

'Perhaps not if it was all a woman knew. Going back only a handful of generations, we are talking mainly about women who couldn't read or write or really do anything without a host of servants. Of course, there were exceptions, the educated daughters of more enlightened men, who were able to establish more equal relationships with their husbands. Women prepared to shout back…like you.'

Willow whirled round. 'Like *me*?' she gasped. 'Jai, I'm one of the most easy-going women you'll ever meet!'

Ice-blue eyes gleamed, sentencing her to stillness. 'Not in my experience…and I like it,' he completed almost as an afterthought.

Was your mother like that and was that why your parents divorced? she suddenly wanted to ask, and her teeth worried at her lower lip before she could make that mistake. 'You…do?'

'If I have expectations of you, naturally you must have expectations of me,' Jai traded, settling his hands to her slender hips in the smouldering silence that seemed to be filtering through the room.

Her heart was banging so hard inside her chest that even catching her breath was a challenge. She gazed up into those extraordinary pale blue eyes welded to her and her heart hammered even faster while a clenching sensation assailed her between her thighs. Sometimes he struck her as so beautiful, he left her breathless. No points for that inane thought, she tried to scold herself, but her body wasn't listening when right at that moment she craved Jai's mouth more than she had ever craved anything. And he gave it to her, hot and hard, exactly what she wanted and needed, the urgency of his lips on hers, the tangling of their tongues, the sudden tightening of his strong arms around her quivering form. She was only dimly aware of her feet leaving the floor and being brought down on the wide low bed.

With an effort, Jai restrained himself from tearing off her clothes like a barbarian because he was burning up for her. It would be different between them this time, the way it *should* have been the night of Hari's conception, he assured himself, snatching in a sustaining breath as he raised her up from the pillows to run down the zip on her dress with the finesse he had somehow forgotten that first time. Stray half-formed thoughts were running through his brain, his father confiding that love in combination with unalloyed lust was a trap of the cruellest order, a trap that had almost destroyed the older man. Jai had always known that he didn't have to worry about such a weakness because he was controlled, cautious, far less naive and trusting than his unfortunate parent had been when he had fallen like a ton of bricks for Jai's mother. Cecilia, the apparent love of his life when he had been twenty-one, Jai conceded cynically, had done that much for him, at least.

Jai lifted the dress over her head and the instant he glimpsed the pouting perfection of her tiny breasts

cupped in something white and intrinsically feminine, the blood ran roaring through his veins. He
gritted his teeth, briefly marvelling at the fierce possessiveness shock-waving through him. Willow was
his wife, the mother of his son, and it was perfectly
natural for him to experience such responses, but it
was something new, which had to be why alarm bells
were shrieking inside his head.

'What's wrong?' Willow asked abruptly.

'Nothing whatsoever, *soniyaa*,' Jai declared,
crushing her mouth under his in a surge of denial at
those alarm bells.

Willow's hands crept up to his shoulders, her anxious gaze pinned to his lean, darkly handsome face.
'Take your shirt off,' she almost whispered.

Jai laughed at her sudden boldness, watching the
colour build in her cheeks as he leant back and loosed
the buttons before peeling it off, enjoying the way
in which her eyes stayed glued to him, recognising
with satisfaction that his bride wanted him as much
as he wanted her. He slid off the bed and began to
strip, deliberately taking his time, reacting to the
synergy between them.

Willow rested back against the pillows, entranced
by the display because she hadn't seen Jai naked
on the night of the funeral, had only caught little
glimpses of him in the dim light filtering into her

bedroom from the landing. And the more he took off clothes-wise, the harder it got for her to breathe through her constricted lungs, because he was a masculine work of art, dark-hair-dusted, lean muscles flexing with his every movement, that long, powerful body of his making her fingers tingle and her breasts swell and tighten inside her bra. She had not known that it was even possible for such a response to assail her and it shook her and then he was coming back to her on the bed, a symphony of lean bronzed masculinity, boldly aroused, and she acknowledged the surge of dampness at the heart of her with burning cheeks.

'What are you blushing about?' Jai husked, sliding a hand to her slender spine to release her bra.

'I liked watching you undress,' she said, as if that was some kind of revelation.

'Let me tell you a secret,' Jai rasped, long fingers curling round a straining nipple. 'I would like watching you undress just as much. I want you as much as you want me…'

'Honestly?' Willow exclaimed as she quivered all over, not quite believing that statement of his.

Jai watched her soft pink mouth open and suddenly he knew he was done with talking, the raw hunger he was struggling to keep within acceptable boundaries overpowering him. He pressed her back against the pillows with the force of his mouth on hers, all the keyed-up ferocious urgency of his need released in that kiss.

Willow squirmed beneath his weight, her hands lifting to clutch at the smooth skin of his strong shoulders, the sheer heat of him an education, a memory, another burning coal to add to the bonfire in her pelvis and the hot, sweet ache stirring there. 'Oh, Jai…' she muttered, pulling her lips free to get some oxygen back into her starved body. 'I don't know what it is that you do to me but it's almost scary.'

That admission so exactly matched Jai's thought about her effect on him that it spooked him, and he buried it fast, too full of need to concentrate on anything else…

CHAPTER SIX

WILLOW QUIVERED AND shook as Jai worked his sensual path down over her squirming body.

She was back in that sensual world where her heart hammered and her body burned with hunger. Her nipples were stiff little points begging for his attention and he dallied there a long time, driving her insane with frustration as her hips rocked on the mattress because she wanted more, *needed* more. 'Jai, *please*…' she gasped, the burning ache throbbing between her thighs more than she could bear.

'This time, we're going to do this *right*,' he ground out, his bright gaze glittering with resolve.

'But there is no right or wrong here…only what we want,' Willow protested, running an exploring hand down over a long, lean expanse of his torso and delving lower, finding him, stroking him, revelling in the satin-smooth hardness of his thrusting manhood, which every cell in her body craved.

Above her, Jai groaned, pushed her hand away, determined not to be deflected by his hunger. But her fingers slid up into his hair to drag him down to her so that she could have his mouth, the deep delve of his tongue, the awesome nip of his teeth along her sensitive lower lip until she was panting for breath and straining up to him, slender thighs wrapping round his narrow hips to hold him there.

Anticipation was licking through Willow in a raging storm of electrifying impulses as she tangled with his tongue, arched her back so that the hard wall of his chest abraded the straining tips of her breasts and ran her hands down his long, lean flanks. Her hunger was racing out of control, the way it always seemed to be with Jai, and she knew she would be mortified later, but just then she couldn't prevent herself from urging him on by every means within her power.

And with a raw expletive, Jai suddenly surrendered without warning. He reached for a condom, dealing with it fast before pushing her back and plunging into her so hard and deep that her neck extended, and her head fell back. Her hair tumbled like rumpled silk across the pillows as she cried out at the raw sweet force of that invasion. He rode her like a runaway horse and she angled up to him in feverish yearning, the wild excitement he fired in her shock-waving through her in a storm of response. It was everything she remembered from that first night, the naked, burning, demanding heat of the violent passion that had brought her alive. There was nothing cool about it, nothing scheduled or controlled. It took over, wiped everything else from her brain and it was, she dimly registered, incredibly addictive.

All the lean power that was Jai drove her to an explosive orgasm that went splintering through her and lit up every nerve ending in her trembling body. In the aftermath of what had felt like a hurricane striking and devastating every sense, she was weak.

'Epic,' Jai breathed with driven honesty, yet still furious with himself for having failed to meet his own standards yet again and for having fallen on her like an animal. Once again he questioned what it was about her that made everything go wrong when it should have been going right *this* time around, and that only put him in mind of something else he was keen to discuss. No time like the present, he decided, tugging her into the shelter of his arms and dropping a kiss on her smooth brow.

'I wish I'd been around when you were carrying Hari,' he admitted.

Surprise winged through Willow and she was so taken aback she sat up to look down at him while simultaneously thinking how very beautiful he was in the sunlight filtering in through the screen. A five o'clock shadow accentuating his superb bone structure, his extraordinarily light black-fringed eyes intent on her. She swallowed hard. 'Yes, well, it's not something we can do much about now.'

'No?' Jai pressed. 'But surely you regret the decisions you made back then.'

Willow stiffened. 'I'm not sure that I do. I did the best I could at the time, and I believed I was doing what was best for both of us.'

Jai sat up with a jerk, his lean, powerful bronzed body tense. 'But you were wrong and *I* missed out on you being pregnant and on Hari's arrival, not to mention every little change in him during the first seven months of his life!' he shot back at her with unexpected ire.

Willow breathed in deep. 'Well, I'm sorry about that,' she muttered uncomfortably, wondering why on earth he was in such a dark mood.

Jai sprang out of bed. 'I don't think you're one bit sorry for having denied me knowledge of my own child!' he fired back at her accusingly.

'Obviously I'm sorry that it upset you but be fair,' Willow urged, disconcerted by that sudden anger of his. 'I honestly didn't realise how much Hari would mean to you or that you would feel so committed to our child once you found out about him.'

'Had it been left to you I would *never* have found out about him!' Jai intoned grimly. 'And I still don't understand what I did or said to deserve that treatment.'

Hugging the sheet round her, Willow had turned very pale, registering that she was finally catching a glimpse of the kind of feelings that Jai had, for whatever reason, concealed from her. He was still furious that she had not told him that she was pregnant. 'It was the way you treated me the morning after that night we spent together,' she told him honestly, for that was the truth of how she had felt at the time.

'Nothing I said justifies your silence when you were carrying my child and in need of my support!' Jai launched back at her without hesitation.

'I managed perfectly well without your support,' Willow snapped back defensively. 'But that morning you condemned me for not telling you that I was a virgin, insisting that you would never have touched me had you known.'

'That was the truth!' Jai sliced in ruthlessly.

'You also said that what we had done was *wrong*,' she reminded him stubbornly. 'And you accused me of still having a teenaged crush on you. I don't know many women who would've wanted to contact a bloke who said stuff like that afterwards.'

'It was your duty to contact me!' Jai interposed icily.

But Willow was only warming up, a keen memory of her feelings back then awakened by his censure. In a sudden movement she bodily yanked the sheet from the bed and left it, but only after wrapping it securely round her, and her colour was high. 'Oh, forget your stupid duty, Jai…it was how you made me *feel* that ruled how I behaved!' she slammed back at him. 'You made it sound like sleeping with me was the biggest *mistake* you had ever made.'

Jai flung his proud dark head back, his sensual mouth flattening into a thin hard line. 'It *was*…'

'Well then, don't be surprised that I didn't get in touch because if that night was such a mistake for you, I was in no mood to tell you that, to add to that mistake, I had also conceived a child that you obviously would not want.'

'Those are two separate issues,' Jai objected. 'My night with you was ill-advised but my child could *never* be a mistake.'

'You see how you're simply changing your wording to make yourself sound better?' Willow condemned angrily and, although she was always slow to anger, she was very, very angry just at that moment because, once again, Jai was making her feel bad. 'Why is it so hard for you to accept that you are not the only one of us to have pride? And you humiliated me that morning and made me feel *awful*. You spent more time talking about my father's books than you did on what had happened between us!'

'That is untrue.'

'No, it is true!' Willow hissed back at him, green eyes blazing. 'I disagreed with what you said about that night and, because I dared to disagree, that was the end of the discussion. You didn't *care* about how you were making me feel.'

Jai registered that a huge argument had blossomed and decided to walk away rather than continue it, continuing it being beneath his dignity in his own mind. He flung open the concealed door in the panelling to the en suite bathroom and closed it firmly behind him, shaken by the fire in his bride and forced to consider her explanation by the essential streak of fairness that he had been raised to respect.

He had *not* humiliated her, he told himself fiercely as he stepped into his luxury rainforest shower, and then he recalled an image of her standing, small and pale and stiff, that morning. Well, *if* he had humiliated her, he had certainly not intended to do so. All he had done was express his feelings concerning their sexual encounter. But he had done so to a former virgin, who could understandably have felt very rejected by such a negative attitude, his conscience slung in with unwelcome timing. He had consciously been trying to distance himself from a chain of events that shamed him, he acknowledged grimly. And she had vehemently disagreed with him and he hadn't known how to handle that, he conceded in grudging addition.

The door of the en suite bathroom opened, Willow finally having realised that the panelling effectively concealed doors into dressing rooms and other facilities only obvious to someone who actually saw a door being used.

'And now you're doing it to me again!' Willow declared angrily from the doorway, incensed by his departure. 'Walking away because I disagree with you!'

In the spacious shower cubicle Jai grimaced. 'I'll join you in a few minutes and we'll talk.'

'Oh, don't bother on my account!' his bride said sharply. 'It's probably jet lag but I'm exhausted and I'm going back to bed for a nap!'

Tears lashing her hurt eyes and angrily blinked back, Willow clambered back into the comfortable bed and curled up into a brooding ball of resentment. Some people didn't like conflict and maybe he was one of them. Obviously, she needed to brush up on her communication skills and stop her temper jumping in first because she was willing to admit that nobody had *ever* made her as angry as Jai could.

He was the very first person she had ever shouted at and in retrospect she was full of chagrin and regret because even she knew that that was not the way to persuade anyone round to a new point of view.

But she just felt so wounded by his outlook because those months pregnant and alone but for Shelley had been very tough. And she truly hadn't appreciated that Jai was still so bone-deep outraged at her failure to tell him that she had conceived. No, he had managed to hide that reaction very effectively until he'd got her to the altar, she reflected bitterly, and only now was she seeing that, for all his appearance of frankness, Jai was much more complex below that surface façade of cool than he seemed and quite capable of nourishing reactions that she'd not even begun to detect.

But then, shouldn't she have expected a few surprises when they were only really getting to know each other now? When it was only a practical marriage rather than one based on love and caring? Well, he definitely had all the caring genes when it came to their son, Willow conceded reluctantly, he just didn't have them for *her*. She felt hollow inside, as if she had been gutted, and a quiver of self-loathing ran through her that she could still be so sensitive to Jai's opinions.

He thought she had let Hari *and* him down by not

informing him that she was pregnant. He would hold it against her to the grave, she thought morosely, suspecting that Jai was as proverbially unforgiving and hard as that vast sandstone fortress above Chandrapur. He expected, he wanted perfection and she had a whole pile of flaws. Jai had flaws too but, unlike her, seemed supremely unaware of them. Of course, she rather suspected that his father had been of a very different nature from hers, not the type to linger on his child's every failing. On that deflating note, Willow fell asleep.

A smiling, dark-skinned face above hers wakened her with a gentle touch on her shoulder.

'I am your maid, Alisha,' the young woman informed her, bobbing her head. 'His Royal Highness the Maharaja will be dining in an hour.'

Dimly, Willow registered that daylight had gone and wondered in dismay how long she had slept, before glancing at her watch and discovering that she had slept for far longer than she had planned.

'I have run a bath for you…but there is a shower… it is your choice,' Alisha added with yet another huge good-natured smile. 'I have also laid out clothes for you.'

Willow was bemused by being awarded that amount of personal attention until it occurred to her that she was receiving it purely as a mark of respect towards Jai's wife, a sort of reflected glory she felt ill-prepared to handle. But she would have to *learn* to handle it, she told herself urgently, because she was living in a formal household crammed with servants and she was always going to be the Maharani of Chandrapur within these walls even if she didn't feel as though she had any true right to such high status and esteem.

'A bath would be great,' she agreed, since it had already been run for her, and she sat up to slide her arms into the silky robe being extended for her use, thinking that Shelley would adore hearing about such luxuries because that kind of personal attention was non-existent in the world in which she and her friend had grown up in. Not so much a world, she ruminated wryly, as the school of hard knocks, which had formed them both from childhood.

Her bathroom was separate from Jai's, Willow realised with a guilty grimace as she sat in her bath surrounded by floating rose petals and some sort of scented oil. No wonder he had seemed startled by her following him in there to confront him yet again, she conceded, heat flushing her cheeks in sudden mortification. No, arguments when she was over-tired and cross were not to be recommended, she conceded ruefully, although she had said nothing that even now, calmer and cooler, she would have been willing to retract.

Her maid had laid out a long dress for her and Willow winced, getting a hint of what her life was expected to be like in the Lake Palace. She was supposed to dress up simply to dine with her bridegroom. Had she been a more conventional new bride, she would've been doing that automatically though, she reflected ironically, an arrow of remorse piercing her that that was not the case between her and Jai. On the surface their marriage might seem normal but underneath it was a sham, bereft of the understanding, love and knowledge that what he had termed 'a normal marriage' would need to thrive.

Alisha directed her downstairs, where Ranjit guided her across the echoing main hallway into yet another splendid room furnished with a formal dining table and chairs. Coloured glass panels portraying a fanciful forest full of fantasy animals decorated the walls and it was wonderfully cool and air-conditioned.

'So, some of this place is air-conditioned,' Willow remarked as Jai strode in, and in stark comparison to her moreover, barefoot and clad with almost laughable informality in an open-necked red shirt and well-fitted designer jeans that outlined his lean hips and long, powerful thighs. As always, he looked

amazing and her breath shortened in her throat as involuntarily she relived the feel of his hot skin below
her stroking fingers, the springy softness of his black
hair and, ultimately, the crashing intoxicating surge
of his mouth on hers.

Burning up with chagrin inside her own skin,
Willow dropped hastily into a chair.

'Yes, those rooms where it was possible without
seriously damaging the décor. If you find our bedroom too warm, just tell me. I will make it possible
there too, but I do not expect us to spend much time
here during the hottest months of the year,' he imparted smoothly, his dark low-pitched voice, richer
than velvet, brushing against skin suddenly pebbling
with goose bumps. 'The summer heat can be unbearable.'

Willow nodded as a wide selection of little bites
was brought in to serve as a first course and Ranjit
carefully indicated the spicy items lest they not be
to her taste, while Jai talked about the local sights
he intended to show her. She tried a sample of fla-
vours while wondering if Jai intended merely to act
as though that argument had not taken place, but,
once the staff had melted away with delivery of their
main course, Jai fell suddenly silent and she glanced
up from her plate anxiously to find those wolfish ice-
blue eyes locked hard to her.

'There is something I must say,' he began, uncharacteristically hesitant in tone. 'There are times when we will perceive events in a dissimilar light because of the different cultures in which we grew up...'

'Obviously,' Willow breathed tightly.

'The morning after we spent that first night together is one of those events. For me, it *was* inexcusably wrong to take a woman's virginity when I was not in a serious relationship with her. I could not treat that as though it was something of no consequence, but I was equally guilty of having made the assumption that you would *not* be so innocent, living in your more liberal society,' he completed levelly.

'Jai, I—' Willow began awkwardly, not having foreseen quite how much of an issue that had genuinely been for him.

'Let me finish,' he urged, topping up her wine glass with a lithe and elegant hand. 'I felt very guilty that day. I was deeply ashamed of my behaviour. I took advantage of you when you were grieving and alone and in need of support.'

'It didn't feel that way to me,' Willow protested, breaking in.

'We are talking about how it felt to be *me* that morning,' Jai reminded her drily. 'I felt like a total bastard, who had seduced an innocent young woman, and clearly how I felt fed into making you feel rejected and insulted…but that result was *not* intentional. I remained sincerely concerned for your well-being, which is why I attempted to see you again a couple of months later, by which time you must've known you were pregnant.'

At the reminder, Willow flushed a discomfited brick red. 'And Shelley lied for me and said she didn't know where I was because she *knew* I didn't want to see you again,' she filled in for him uneasily. 'I'm sorry but that was just how I felt back then. I was a bit naive. I was feeling well and I thought I would manage fine without you. Before I forget, can I ask you something off-topic?'

His winged ebony brows drew together in a frown at that query. 'You can ask me anything although I cannot always guarantee an answer.'

'Why did I have to get all dressed up in a long fancy gown when you're wearing jeans and no shoes?'

And the tension still thick round the table just evaporated then and there as Jai flung his handsome dark head back and laughed with disconcerting appreciation of that simple question. Raking a long-fingered brown hand through his silky black hair, he surveyed her with amusement still glittering like stardust in his bright black-lashed eyes. 'I can only assume that it was my mother's practice or my grandmother's practice to get "all dressed up" for dinner because that is how long it has been since this palace had a mistress. Your maid will have been given advice on what you would want to wear for such an occasion and, since you are English, it may well date back to the years of the British Raj,' he warned her with a wide smile. 'And be generations out of date. You don't need to dress up for dinner for my benefit. You can wear whatever you like, *soniyaa.*'

That smile of his and the endearment on top of the explanation he had carefully outlined melted that hard little knot that had formed in Willow's chest earlier that day. Jai was trying and she recognised that, respected him for it, *liked* him for it. But at the other end of the scale she was wondering what other misunderstandings would crop up when there were such basic differences between their outlooks on life. Even so, stifling that anxious thought, she smiled back at him, shaken to discover how fast she wanted him again, as if that afternoon of passion had only been a dream.

'This evening I will show you around what remains of your new home and tomorrow we will go out and explore,' Jai promised her lazily.

And the week that followed was full of enjoyment, occasional challenges and surprises and the beginning of a fascination with her surroundings that rooted deep. There was the ancient old gardener who brought her flowers every day, and the cook who had a burning desire to know what her favourite foods were, and the sharing of playtimes with Hari and his father, so that a lifestyle that at first had seemed strange became her new normal. Hari was always surrounded by loving carers and it was not unusual to hear his chuckles as he was rocked in a solid-silver nursery swing that had rocked his ancestors for generations and which really should have been in a museum.

Willow visited the Hindu temple and the white marble park of elaborate ancestral tombs that overlooked the holy lake. She accepted garlands and blessings and small gifts for Hari as well as her share of the awe that Jai's mere presence inspired amongst the locals. She posed for photos for the local journalists, who were much more respectful than those they had encountered at the airport.

She learned that English was widely spoken and became less intimidated by strangers, her confidence growing at the warm welcome she received everywhere. She explored the massive old fortress on the cliffs above the city, bowled over by its magnificent décor and huge rooms, with Jai by her side sharing funny stories about his heritage, which no guide could ever have equalled. And she saw a tiger in the wild for the first time, ironically not on the mini safari in an open-topped SUV that Jai had taken her on, but from the shaded dining terrace she watched the animal slink in his glorious orange and black striped coat out of the jungle to pad down at his leisure to drink at the edge of the lake.

By day they explored the sights but by night, mostly, they explored each other, she reflected with a wanton and slightly self-conscious little wriggle of recollection. She couldn't keep her hands off Jai, and it seemed to be a case of a mutual chemical reaction. Jai electrified her every time he touched her, but when he had pressed her down in one of those reading nooks in the library that day, and possessed her with uninhibited passion in one of their most exciting encounters to date, she had realised afterwards, by his faint but perceptible discomfiture, that Jai wasn't in control either.

Jai was pondering that problem for himself in his office. He had been spending too much time with his wife and not enough time working, he censured himself, well aware that he was sidestepping the real issue nagging at him. He had married her for his son's sake, he reminded himself impatiently. He had planned on a perfectly civilised but essentially detached and sophisticated partnership in marriage, in which both of them nourished their own interests and friendships. He had never planned on hot, sweaty, wildly exciting naked encounters in every secluded corner of his home. He had never planned to keep her awake half the night in the marital bed to the extent that she regularly fell asleep in the afternoon heat, exhausted by his demands. Nobody needed to warn Jai that he was already in the grip of the overpowering lust that he had been warned against many times.

And that acknowledgement disturbed Jai on every level. He didn't do love; he flatly refused to do love. He was a great believer in moderation in all things. He had, after all, grown up with the tragic evidence of what love could do to a man, not to mention his own disillusionment at the hands of his former fiancée, Cecilia. Love, however, had totally broken his father, a strong man, a good man, an intelligent man, yet none of those strengths had saved him from the consequences of losing the wife he had adored. His father's depressions, loneliness, bitterness, his inability to replace that lost wife with even a female friend, had taught Jai how dangerously harmful those softer emotions could be for a man when it came to a woman.

He didn't want the stress of that complication with Willow: he was determined not to *need* her, to look for her when she wasn't there or to allow her to sink so deeply into the fabric of his everyday life that she became more important than she should be. Liking, kindness and respect were absolutely all that were required from him as a husband and anything beyond that would be madness...a madness that he wouldn't touch.

CHAPTER SEVEN

A WEEK AFTER Jai reached that decision, and unhappily warding off her low spirits as a result of that decision, Willow was dealing with the post her social secretary had gathered for her to peruse.

Yes, she was tickled pink by the idea that she could possibly require a social secretary. Only after she had seen the pile of invitations, congratulatory letters and wedding gifts in Samaira's small office had she realised that she had been ridiculously naive not to appreciate that Jai's position with an international charity foundation, his local role as a former ruler and his recent marriage would not also make demands on *her*.

'And there was *this*,' the tiny, beautiful Samaira finally declared, sliding a sheet of paper across the desk and rising at the same time to leave the library. 'It's an email that arrived on the Maharaja's historical website and I was given it by his PA, Mitul. He took the liberty of printing it out, which I hope was correct,' she added hopefully. 'We felt that the enquiry was for you and best given to you.'

Surprised by that seemingly unnecessarily detailed explanation, Willow frowned and glanced down at the paper, looking first at the signature. Milly St John, a name that meant nothing whatsoever to her. She studied the couple of lines in the message before comprehension gripped her with sudden dismay.

As you have recently married my son and are the mother of my grandson, I would be very grateful if you would agree to meet with me alone and in private at my hotel in Chandrapur on the seventeenth.'

Willow paled, because it was an extraordinary request from a woman that Jai would not even discuss. It was also a hot potato that had passed quickly from hand to hand, the staff probably striving to work out the best way to deal with it since Jai's aversion to anything relating to his mother was clearly well known. And Samaira was right, it *was* an invitation for Willow but undoubtedly not one of which Jai would approve.

'Thank you,' Willow said quietly, keen not to embellish the staff grapevine by commenting on an email that had very probably already caused a wave of gossip and speculation.

And while she was pondering that problem and what to do about it, she too left the library and wandered down to the far end of the palace in the direction of the suite of offices that had been neatly tailored from what had once been staff quarters. There she hesitated, uncertain that she even wanted to raise such a prickly topic, for in recent days Jai had become progressively more elusive. Yes, she had accepted that he would have to return to work, but she had not appreciated quite how much business would occupy his time. He usually joined her for dinner but rarely for breakfast or lunch, invariably rising before her and retiring after she had. She was relieved, however, that in spite of that relentless schedule he had still made time for their son, even if any notion of making time for *her* seemed to have died a total death after that first glorious week together.

Willow understood, however, that he was very busy, and she wasn't the clingy type. She didn't need him to fill the daylight hours when she had Hari to occupy her, a beautiful garden and an entire library of books, but she couldn't help thinking that Jai was treating her rather like a new and shiny novelty whose initial lustre had quickly worn off and ended up boring him instead. On that note, she turned her steps in another direction and decided to ask him what she felt she needed to ask him over dinner instead.

Later, Jai strolled out to the big domed terrace that was shaded throughout the day and cool. Willow sipped her wine and savoured his long-legged grace and sheer bronzed beauty with his black-lashed arctic-blue eyes glittering. A little quiver ran through her slender length, her breasts peaking almost painfully below the bodice of the sundress she wore, a clenching sensation tightening deep in her pelvis so that colour flared up in her cheeks. 'Hello, stranger,' she heard herself say even though she had not intended to make any comment on his recent inaccessibility.

Jai lifted a black brow in query, as if that greeting had totally taken him aback.

'I haven't seen you since I woke to see you walking out of our bedroom yesterday morning,' Willow pointed out, watching the faint rise of colour that scored his exotic cheekbones with curiosity. 'Hey, I'm not complaining. I'm just pointing it out.'

Disconcerted by that statement, Jai breathed. 'Has it really been that long? I'm sorry but I had to attend a board meeting for the foundation last night. It ran late and I didn't want to disturb you, so I used another room.'

'I think you need to learn to delegate more,' Willow responded with determined lightness. 'It's not healthy for anyone to be working twenty-four-seven.'

Jai gritted his teeth, belatedly recognising in that moment that he had gone to quite absurd lengths to avoid his wife for the sin of attracting him too strongly. He dimly wondered if there was a streak of insanity somewhere in his family genes. What had seemed like such a good idea a week earlier had now blurred and become questionable. In the midst of scanning her tiny slender figure in a sunflower-yellow dress, which accentuated the strawberry-blond waves curling round her piquant face and framed her catlike green eyes, he reckoned that no normal man would have behaved as he had done: resisting his beautiful wife's allure as though she were both toxic and dangerous.

He could only assume that the literal act of getting married had afflicted him with some very weird and deferred form of cold feet. All to prove some kind of point to himself? That he was in control? And able to *wreck* his marriage before it even got off the ground? He breathed in deeply, recognising in bewilderment that his usual rational outlook inexplicably seemed to always send him in the wrong direction with Willow.

'Even with the party scheduled, next week won't

be half as frantic for me,' Jai assured her hurriedly as Ranjit poured the wine and retreated.

'Good,' Willow replied with a smile that lit up her face like sunshine. 'But the party event has also given me some questions I feel I *have* to ask you about your background.'

Jai tensed. 'My…background?'

'I feel awkward about asking but I feel I should know the basic facts, because I will be mixing with your relatives, who presumably already know those facts, and I don't want to trip up in my ignorance and say anything that sounds stupid,' Willow outlined, trotting out the excuse she had prepared and reddening hotly because simply telling him the truth would have come much more naturally to her.

Yet in her heart of hearts she had already guessed that Jai would absolutely forbid her to have anything to do with his mother, but Lady Milly was *her* mother-in-law and Hari's grandmother and, although she was a stranger, Willow still felt that she surely ought to have the right to form her own opinion.

'Facts about what?' Jai prompted.

'About why your parents broke up, about why your mother left you behind,' she murmured tightly, guilt still jolting through her in waves.

'My mother is the daughter of an English duke, which is still virtually all I know about her. The marriage didn't last long and ended in divorce…' Jai compressed his sensual mouth into a flat bitter line '…*because* apparently she believed that her alliance with an Indian and the birth of a mixed-race child were adversely affecting her social status.'

'That's weird… I mean, if she believed that why would she have married your father in the first place?' Willow pressed with a furrowed brow.

'I have never had a conversation with her, consequently I don't know,' Jai admitted flatly.

'You've never even *met* her?' Willow exclaimed in disbelief.

'I don't think you could call it a meeting… I did run into her once quite unexpectedly at a public event and she pretty much cut me dead. Her second husband and children were with her,' Jai explained, and his strong bone structure might have been formed with steel beneath his olive skin, his forbidding cast of features as revealing of his feelings on that occasion as the ice in his gaze.

'That was unforgivable,' Willow conceded, shocked and unhappy on his behalf.

Jai frowned. 'Of course, she did attempt to come back from that very low point. Shortly afterwards, she came to my London home in an attempt to see me, but I had her turned away. In fact, there were several attempts, but I have no desire to either see

or speak to her. She sent letters as well, which I returned unopened. At this stage in my life and with
my father dead, I see no reason to waste time on her.'

Willow, however, saw with great clarity that Jai
had been cruelly hurt by his mother's twin rejections and that, no matter what he said in that mea-
sured and cool voice of his, he was still scarred by
the damage his mother's abandonment had inflicted.
And so stubborn too, so set in his views that he had
completely rejected the olive branch and the explana-
tions that the woman had tried to offer. Of course, in
such circumstances that was his right, she accepted
ruefully, resolving in that moment not to interfere
on behalf of a woman who, it seemed, was a most
undeserving cause. She herself would sooner have
cut off her arm than walk away from Hari.

'I'm sorry I asked,' she told him truthfully. 'I can't
blame you for feeling the way you do about her.'

And she decided not to mention the personal approach that had been made to her by his mother,
which would undoubtedly only annoy Jai and where
was the point in that? It would be yet another wound-
ing reminder of the wretched woman that he didn't
need. No, she would stay safely uninvolved in a matter that was none of her business and ignore that
email.

Jai strolled round the courtyard garden with her

after dinner, but Willow was quiet and withdrawn in receipt of that unexpected attention. After all, she really didn't know where she stood with Jai any more. Her first week with him had been magical and then he had virtually vanished, and with that vanishing act all her insecurities had been revived. Why would he want to spend time with her when he had never really wanted to marry her in the first place? How could she feel neglected when she had known beforehand that she was entering a marriage without love? How could she even complain?

'I screwed up this week,' Jai declared, in a driven undertone.

In silence, Willow shrugged a stiff shoulder and hovered below the ancient banyan tree in the centre of the garden, which sheltered a sacred shrine much revered by the staff. '*I* didn't complain about anything,' she reminded him with pride, studying him with clear green eyes.

Her problem, though, was that Jai was gorgeous, in whatever light and in whatever clothing. Nothing detracted from his sheer magnificence: the luxuriant black hair, the chiselled cheekbones and flawless skin, the stunning ice-blue eyes and the dramatic lashes that surrounded them, and he had an equally beautiful body, she allowed, her face warming at that unarguable acknowledgement. Unfortunately for her, on every physical plane, Jai drew her like a magnet. One certain look, one smile and she was all over him like a stupid rash and that both infuriated her and made her feel weak and foolish. After the week she had endured of being ignored in *and* out of bed, she knew that in reality she meant very little to Jai and it felt degrading to still be attracted to a man who could simply switch off and forget her very existence.

The real source of Willow's frustration, however, was, undeniably, that she had no idea what was going on inside his head. She was beginning to wonder if it was possible that, aside of sex, Jai hadn't a clue how to behave in the sort of relationship that a marriage required. The first week with him had been heavenly and she had been so happy with him that she had practically floated, but the past week of being ignored had been a sobering wake-up call that hurt her self-esteem. One minute she had seemed as necessary to him as the air he needed to breathe, the next she had become the invisible woman.

'I will spend more time with you from now on,' Jai intoned with deadly seriousness.

Willow paled and walked on down the path. 'Don't push yourself,' she heard herself say curtly, the colour of embarrassment stinging her cheeks.

'It's not like that,' Jai assured her levelly, lifting

a long-fingered brown hand to rest on her shoulder with an intimacy she resented because it reminded her too much of those carnal, expert hands sliding over her body.

'Well, going by the past week, it *is* like that,' Willow replied, squaring her slight shoulders and stepping away to break that physical connection. 'You don't know what you want from me…apart from the obvious…*sex*,' she condemned between gritted teeth. 'And this past week, not even that. You married me and I don't think you know what to do with me now that you've got what you *said* you wanted!'

Evidently stunned by that disconcerting burst of frankness, Jai briefly froze, his darkly handsome features taut.

'Goodnight, Jai,' Willow murmured quietly and walked back indoors, for once proud of herself for not succumbing to the sexual infatuation that had entrapped her into something that felt disturbingly like an obsession.

Why was she feeling like that? Even not seeing Jai hurt, never mind not being touched by him or talking to him. Somehow, he had sparked off a hunger inside her that tugged at her through every hour of the day and she resented him for reducing her to that needy level. He should've started their marriage on cooler, more detached terms if that was how he intended it to be. Instead he had given her deceptive false messages and had shaken her up from the inside out.

Well, she was not some pushover for him to lift and literally *lay* whenever he fancied, she was strong, independent and nobody's fool, she reminded herself doggedly. She might not have been her father or Jai's intellectual equal, but had always been shrewd when it came to people and the often confusing difference between what they said and what they actually did. She knew how to look after herself even if she had once been foolish enough to succumb to a one-night stand with Jai.

Tense from that encounter in the garden, she went upstairs to look in on Hari as he slept, safe and smiling in the baby equivalent of the Land of Nod, probably dreaming of being rocked in a silver swing by devoted handmaidens while being fed ambrosia. If only life were so simple for her, she thought wryly. Lifting her head high, she scolded herself for that downbeat thought. She had Hari and life was very good for him. She had health and security too. There *was* no excuse for feeling that her life lacked anything. In that mood, she scooped up silk pyjamas from her cavernous collection of lingerie and went for a bath.

She was lying back on her padded bath pillow engaged in aggressively counting the many blessings she had to be grateful for when, with a slight knock and only a momentary hesitation, the door opened to frame Jai on the threshold, tall and lean, dark and hazardous, pale eyes glittering like stars framed by black velvet. Willow jerked up in surprise and hugged her knees with defensive hands, feeling invaded. 'I didn't ask you to come in.'

Jai tilted his dark head back, a dangerous glint in his bright gaze. 'What makes you think I need permission to speak to my wife?'

Willow lifted a pale brow. 'Courtesy?'

Jai closed the door and sank down on the edge of the bath, deliberately entering her safe space. 'Courtesy won't get us anywhere we want to travel right now.'

Willow lifted her chin. 'Then get out of here... *now*!' she challenged.

Disturbingly, Jai laughed and trailed a forefinger through the rose petals swirling round her knees. 'I don't think so. I am where I *want* to be. If you can be direct, so can I. I want you.'

At the sound of that declaration the blood drummed up through Willow's body like an adrenalin boost. 'Since...*when*?' she mocked.

'I can't switch it off. With you, it's a primal and very basic urge and it hurts to deny it.' Jai's fingertip glided up out of the water to slowly stroke the soft underside of her full lower lip and her heart hammered at an insane rate.

'So, why did you?' she whispered unevenly.

'I thought I should. I don't know why. I don't like feeling out of control,' Jai admitted thickly, his mesmeric gaze holding hers with sheer force of will. 'And you often make me feel out of control...'

And a huge wave of heat that had nothing to do with the temperature of the water shot up through Willow. Her brain was blurring as though it had been enveloped in fog. She could feel her own heart thrumming inside her chest, the tautness of her pointed nipples, the pool of liquefying warmth at her core, but she couldn't think straight and when he angled his mouth down to hers, her mouth opened, only anticipation guiding her. His mouth on hers was like paraffin thrown on a bonfire, shooting multicoloured sparks of heat through every fibre, and only a slight gasp escaped her throat when he lifted her, dripping, out of the water and melded his lips to hers again with all the urgency she had dreamt of.

'I'm soaking wet! This wasn't supposed to happ—' she began, common sense struggling to get a look-in as he laid her down on the bed and arranged her like some ancient sacrifice on an altar.

'Shush, *soniyaa*,' Jai breathed hungrily against her mouth and she was vaguely aware of him peeling off his clothes in the midst of kissing her, but she was too connected to the sheer power surge of his urgency to make even the smallest complaint.

He ran his palms slowly down over her smooth body as if reacquainting himself with her slender contours and she shivered, every skin cell primed for more, her breath trapped in her throat as if breathing might prevent the excitement already licking through her. He slid down the length of her, all lithe bronzed grace and tenacity, his skin hot where it brushed hers, his bold arousal brushing her stomach, filling her with heat and the kind of wanting that burned. He tipped her thighs back, settled his lips to the most sensitive part of her quivering body and slowly, surely, with his mouth and his wickedly knowing fingers, proceeded to drive her out of her mind with throbbing waves of pleasure. She squirmed and then she writhed, unable to stay in control and flying involuntarily into an intense climax, with his name breaking from her tongue and then the taste of herself on her lips as he kissed her with ferocious demand and settled over her.

From that shattering point on, it was as it always was between them: wild. He plunged into her with a growl of satisfaction and she gasped in delight from the first thrust, the delicious stretching of her tingling body, the sleek hardness of his body driving over and in hers and the raw sexual connection that destroyed her every inhibition. He flipped her over onto her hands and knees, pressing her down, entering her powerfully and deeply again, making every sense sing in high-voltage response. Sobs of excitement were wrenched from her convulsing throat as another climax seized hold of her and shock-waved through her with an intensity that wiped her out. She flopped flat on the bed like a puppet who'd had her strings cut, smiling dizzily into the silk bed cover at his shout of completion, knowing that never in her life before had she dreamt of that much excitement and that much drowning pleasure.

'No more starting work at dawn, no more late nights,' Jai breathed with ragged resolution as he turned her limp length over and back into contact with the hot, damp heat of his body, sealing her there with both arms, his hands smoothing her slender back in a soothing motion.

'You're going to delegate?' she whispered with effort because it was a challenge to kick her brain into gear again.

'With the foundation, yes. My life has changed now that I have you and Hari and I need to adapt,' he murmured, setting the edge of his teeth into the exact spot on the slope of her neck that drove her crazy and making her jerk against him. 'In many ways.'

And Willow was satisfied by those assurances. He was making a major effort. He hadn't approached her simply for sex. No, he had recognised that change would be required from both of them if their marriage was to survive and that was good, wasn't it? She shouldn't *still* want more, should she? She couldn't understand the lingering hollow sensation in her chest, particularly when her body was already warming up again to the stimulation of his.

Of course, he wasn't going to start talking about emotions—that was a female thing, wasn't it? Concentrate on the positives, she told herself sternly. Both of them were finding their way in a new and very different situation as parents and partners. Of course, there would be misunderstandings and clashes along the way. All that should really matter was that Jai cared enough to put in the work to keep their relationship ticking over.

Obviously, he was unlikely to ever give her the kind of rapturous reception he gave Hari every time he lifted his son into his arms. She had seen that look, that intense emotion he hid around her and, if she was honest, had envied her son, who had inspired love in his father practically at first sight. But she was only human and it was normal to make comparisons, even if they were unwise comparisons, because love and devotion had featured nowhere in their agreement. Even worse, logic warned her that Jai, a tough businessman to his fingertips, would stick exactly to the deal he had made with her.

She didn't have what it took to inspire Jai with romantic feelings. That had been made clear to her the morning after their first night together. Yes, he had visited to check on her a couple of months later but that had only been a knee-jerk sense of responsibility she owed to his friendship with her late father. It had not related to her *personally*. Her main attraction for Jai was self-evidently the passion that virtually set fire to their bedsheets and she was beginning to recognise that she ought not to be turning her nose up at that rather lowering truth when it might well prove to be the glue that kept their marriage afloat in the future.

Or would familiarity breed contempt? She shivered, wondering why her thoughts continually took a negative direction around Jai. What was the matter with her? Why couldn't she simply be content with what they had? Why was she always seeking...*more*?

CHAPTER EIGHT

JAI LOOKED MAGNIFICENT.

Indeed, Willow was flooded by distinctly sensual and, admittedly, superficial impressions of Jai garbed in traditional Maharaja dress in readiness for the party that would introduce her as his wife to his family and friends. In the black and silver frogged silk tunic and pants, he took her breath away. In fact, virtually everything about the pomp and ceremony of the occasion and their surroundings was having the same effect on her. His grandfather's art deco palace was a sumptuous building with soaring marble columns and ceilings, glittering Venetian glass chandeliers and intricately designed marble floors and even the furniture and the grounds around the building matched that splendid classic elegance, but Jai had been quite correct: it was too grand a place for mere comfort.

As soon as they had arrived in their finery and in

advance of the party, official photographs had been taken in the Greek-style marble temple in the centre of the lawns. They had leant against pillars, posed on the layers of steps, looked pensively into each other's eyes until she'd succumbed to an uncontrollable bout of giggles and then she had twirled in her gown for the photographer to show off the full skirt of her gorgeous dress.

She had felt remarkably like a Bollywood movie actress and Jai had told her that all photos taken for special occasions had a dash of that spirit in India. When she had asked Jai if she should don a sari to blend in better at the party, Jai had only laughed before informing her that many of their guests would be European and that some of his countrywomen would dress traditionally while others would wear the latest Western fashion, that, in actuality, however she chose to dress would be acceptable.

Willow had picked a spectacular ball gown out of her crammed wardrobe, a brilliant cerise-pink shade much favoured by Rajasthani women. The finest lace covered her shoulders and upper arms, the style closely tailored to her slender figure down to the hip and then flaring out in volume into the beaded silk skirt. It was one of those ridiculously beautiful fairy-tale dresses that made a woman feel like a million dollars and to complement it she had worn very high heels. In addition, Jai had brought her a glorious emerald and diamond necklace and earrings, which had belonged to his grandmother, as well as having gifted her a diamond bracelet and a gold and diamond watch that very same week. It was little wonder that she kept on wanting to pinch herself to see if she was still living in the real world because, only weeks earlier, she could never have dreamt that such incredible luxury would ever feature in her life.

In the echoing marble hall, there was a huge display of wedding gifts and they wandered around examining them. Willow was disconcerted by the large amount of jewellery she had been given, gleaming gold necklaces and armbands and earrings, and there were even some pieces for Jai, which he assured her with a groan that he would never wear. She strolled up to him when he was holding something in his hand and signalling his hovering PA, Mitul, to ask him a question.

With an exclamation in his own language he set the ornate little box down again in haste, his sensual mouth compressing. Curious, Willow scooped it up. 'What is it?' she asked.

'An eighteenth-century *inro*—an ornamental box in which Japanese men used to carry seals or medicine. I collect them,' he told her in a curt undertone.

'A very good friend must've given it,' Willow assumed, because everything on the tables struck her as valuable. 'But why are you annoyed? Was it an unsuitable gift from the friend concerned?'

'In my opinion, yes,' Jai conceded crisply. 'The giver is my ex-fiancée, Cecilia.'

'The one that ditched you?' Willow gasped in surprise.

All of a sudden, Jai grinned, the tension in his lean, handsome features evaporating again. 'You're no diplomat, are you, *jaani*?'

Willow reddened because she knew that she hadn't been tactful. 'I know nothing about her…but what upsets you about the present?'

'That I have only just learned that she and her husband have been invited to the party. Odds are that she won't come. But if she does, it's entirely *my* fault that she received an invite,' he acknowledged in exasperation. 'I told Mitul to use the same guest list for my friends that was used ten years ago at a party I held here. But he didn't work for me back then and he wouldn't have recognised the significance of her name. Of course, I should've checked the list myself.'

'It's a very big party,' she reminded him. 'Will it really matter if she turns up?'

Jai shrugged, a brooding expression etched to his flawless features, his wolf eyes veiled by his lashes.

'Her presence would be inappropriate at a reception being staged for my bride's introduction.'

'Well, if she turns up, *I'm* not bothered,' Willow confided, reckoning that she only had curiosity to be satisfied in such a scenario. 'It must be almost ten years since you were with her. I have the vaguest memory of Dad mentioning your wedding being cancelled and I was so young back then that it feels like a very, *very* long time ago.'

'You have a wonderfully welcome ability to ignore developments or mistakes that would enrage and distress other women I have known,' Jai remarked, his pale glittering gaze fully focussed on her as he smiled down at her appreciatively.

Her heartbeat sped up so much she almost clamped her hand to her chest, and she swallowed back the dryness in her throat. 'But that doesn't mean that I'm not nosy,' she told him playfully, fighting her susceptibility to that smile with all her might, for he might have the power of command over her every sense but she didn't want him influencing her brain into the bargain. 'Tell me about her...'

'Some other time,' Jai parried, closing down that informational avenue without hesitation, the hand he had braced lightly against her spine urging her forward to greet the couple who had entered. 'Our first arrivals...congratulations, Jivika! How did you get your husband out the door this early?' he asked with a grin, clearly on warm, relaxed terms with the older couple.

'I thought your bride might enjoy some support at a family event like this and, like most men, I doubt it even occurred to you that this *is* a rather intimidating event for a newcomer,' the older woman said drily to Jai as she walked towards Willow and extended her hand. 'I'm Jai's aunt, Jivika, his father's sister. I'll give you the lowdown on the family members to avoid and those you can afford to encourage,' she promised with a surprisingly warm smile lighting up her rather stern features.

'Jivika!' her husband scolded.

Jai just laughed. 'I could put my wife in no safer hands. Willow, be warned… Jivika was a leading barrister in London and retirement is challenging for her.'

'Only during Indian winters,' his aunt corrected. 'The rest of the year we live in London.'

Willow was grateful for the older woman's assistance as a slow steady flood of guests flowed through the giant doors and drinks were served in the vast drawing room. 'Grandad was *so* pretentious,' Jivika said of her surroundings.

And her commentaries on various relatives were equally entertaining. Willow got used to asking Jai's

aunt to identify guests and when she saw her husband
deeply engaged in conversation with a tall, shapely
blonde, beautiful enough to pass as a supermodel,
she couldn't resist asking who she was.

'Cecilia Montmorency. What's she doing here?'
Jivika asked bluntly in turn.

Jolted by that name, Willow explained the mistake
on the guest list while becoming disconcerted that
Cecilia was constantly touching Jai's arm and laughing up into his face in a very intimate manner. She
registered that she was not quite as safe from jealous
possessiveness as she had cheerfully assumed. But
then how could she be? Jai must have *loved* Cecilia
to want to marry at the age of twenty-one, and love
was a binding emotion that people didn't tend to forget, not to mention a deeper layer of commitment that
Willow had lacked in her marriage from the outset.

'You're seeing a not-so-merry divorcee on the
prowl for her next meal ticket,' Jivika commented.
'It must be galling to know that she once dumped
one of the richest men in the world.'

It was Willow's turn to stare and exclaim, *'Jai's...?'*

His aunt smiled. 'I like that you didn't know but
you can bet your favourite shoes that Cecilia knows
what he's worth down to the last decimal point.'

Willow guiltily cherished the older woman's take
on Jai's ex as a gold-digger and, relaxing more and

more in her company, she became more daring and asked about Jai's mother, asking what sort of woman she had been that she could walk away from her child.

'Been listening to Jai's version of reality, I assume?' Jivika shot her a wry glance. 'Jai was indoctrinated by my brother from an early age. Milly *didn't* walk away from her son by choice. My brother, Rehan, fought her through the courts for years and succeeded in denying her access to her son, even in the UK while Jai was at school there. In the end she gave up—the woman really didn't have much choice after the legal system in both countries had repeatedly failed her.'

Stunned by that very different version of events, Willow studied the other woman in disbelief. 'Why didn't you tell Jai?'

Jivika spread her hands and sighed, 'At first, loyalty to my much-loved but misguided brother and, since his death, no desire to raise sleeping dogs and upset Jai. He's astute. He's capable of making his own decisions. It's not my place to interfere and he could hate me for it.'

Willow swallowed hard, thinking of the judgements she had made about Jai's mother simply by listening to *his* opinion of his mother's behaviour. That he might not know the truth had not once occurred to her. Now she was barely able to imagine what it would be like for him to learn that the father he had loved and respected had lied to him for years on the same subject and she fully understood his aunt's unwillingness to intervene. Jai deserved to know the truth and yet who would want to be the one to *tell* him? she thought ruefully.

Sher joined them and was about to move on when a question from Jivika revealed that Willow had trained as a garden designer. His handsome features sparked with sudden interest and he turned back to say, 'I'll call over in a few days and put a project in front of you…*if* you're interested? I have a garden to restore.'

'I'd be happy to offer advice but I haven't had a huge amount of working experience,' Willow admitted ruefully, because Hari's impending birth and her need to earn money had forced her to put her potential career on a back burner.

'Good enough for me,' Sher told her reassuringly. 'What counts is not the number of projects you have completed but whether or not you have the eye and the skill and can interpret my preferences.'

'I'll let you decide that,' Willow said, colouring a little with relief, encountering Jai's bright shrewd gaze as he joined them and swept her onto the dance floor with the quite unnecessary explanation that it was expected of them.

'You seem to have managed beautifully without me by your side,' Jai observed.

Willow looked up at him, wondering why she couldn't decide whether that statement was supposed to be a positive or negative comment. Her nose wrinkled and she smiled. 'Having your aunt by my side was like having an entire army backing me,' she confided with helpless honesty.

Jai laughed out loud. 'I'm very fond of Jivika,' he admitted. 'She was particularly stellar when I was homesick in London as a child. Of course, she and my father were very close.'

Not quite as close as they could've been, Willow reflected, thinking of that exchange relating to Jai's mother, before conceding that the Singh family dynamic was vastly different from anything she had ever seen before, because even his family treated Jai with the reverence his status as Maharaja commanded, a bred-in-the-bone awe that his father must have enjoyed as well. Such men might not have the right to rule any longer in a republic, but the people still viewed them as being very special and unquestionably royal. Every month Jai held an audience at which any of his father's former subjects could approach him for advice or assistance of any kind and he still saw it as his duty to give that attention to those in need.

'So, my family and friends haven't been as intimidating for you as Jivika feared?' Ice-blue eyes inspected her face with unmistakeable concern.

Touched by that consideration, Willow shifted a little closer to him and his arms tightened round her before his hands smoothed down to the gentle curve of her hips. 'No, everyone's been wonderfully welcoming. How was Cecilia?' she dared.

The faintest colour fired the exotic slant of Jai's hard cheekbones. 'Unchanged. She has one of those amazingly bubbly personalities that always charms, even though she's been through what sounds like a pretty brutal divorce. I was surprised that her arrival and her approach didn't annoy me more...but then we broke up a long time ago and, looking back, I'm prepared to admit that at that age I was more of a boy than a man. It's time to forgive and forget.'

Willow hadn't been prepared to detect quite that much enthusiasm on the topic of the ex who had jilted him. Dimly, she supposed it was healthier that Jai wasn't bitter and had clearly long since moved on from that period of his life.

'She'll probably visit us. She's gasping to meet Hari,' Jai added lightly.

'Why on earth would *she* want to meet Hari?'

Willow demanded with an astonishment she wasn't quick enough to hide.

'Because he's my son and possibly because she can't have children of her own,' Jai proffered, his intonation cool and on the edge of critical, his far too clever ice-blue eyes locking to her flushed face, his lean, strong length stiffening a little against her as he moved her expertly around the floor. 'That's why her husband divorced her. Apparently, he's desperate for a son and heir.'

Willow's brain kicked into gear again. 'How very sad,' she remarked, literally stooping to the level of *forcing* fake sympathy into her voice. 'But I thought she had come only for the wedding.'

'No, seems she's doing a tour of Rajasthan while she's here,' Jai interposed, the tension in his lean, powerful frame dissipating again. 'I said I'd draw up a list of sites she shouldn't miss…'

As if there weren't at least a thousand tour guides for hire in Chandrapur alone, Willow thought sourly, because tourism was a huge source of income in the Golden Triangle, as the area was often described.

'I'm sure she would find that very helpful,' Willow commented blithely, annoyance with him, even greater annoyance with Cecilia and a tumble of confusing emotions raining down on her from all sides. Jai was teaching her to lie like a trooper, as the saying went, she conceded guiltily, but nowhere in their relationship was there any given right for her to make a fuss on such a score as a too-friendly ex-girlfriend. They had a marriage of convenience, not a love match, such as he had once almost achieved with Cecilia.

There was no avoiding the obvious: she was jealous and possessive of the man she had married. Disquiet gripped her. When had that happened? How had she failed to notice such responses creeping up on her? In the midst of her turmoil, Jai kissed her, one hand on her shoulder, one framing her face, and she fell into that kiss like a drowning swimmer plunged fathoms deep without warning. Her body lit up like a firework display, nipples tightening, pelvis clenching as if he had done something much more intimate than press his sensual mouth to hers. But then Jai had a way with a kiss that could burn through her like a flame. Like honey being heated, she was warming, melting, pressing closer to the allure of his hard, muscular physique, no detail of him concealed by the fine silk he wore. An arrow of satisfaction pierced Willow then, for Jai might have talked fondly about his ex but it was still *his wife* who turned him on.

'We'll have to stay on the floor,' Jai growled in her ear. 'I'm not presentable right now.'

Willow chuckled, her cheeks colouring, for over the past week she had learned that she and Jai always seemed to scorch each other when they touched. She wanted to reach up and kiss him again, more deeply and for longer, but she resisted the urge, reminding herself that they were surrounded by people.

Later, Jivika and her husband were leaving when the older woman signalled her, and Willow walked over to her with a wide smile. 'It occurs to me that a wife who is loved could tackle that difficult subject we discussed earlier,' she murmured sibilantly. 'If you break the ice, I will be happy to share all that I know with my nephew.'

Willow maintained her smile with difficulty, but she could feel the blood draining from her face because she was *not* a loved wife, not even close to it, she acknowledged painfully, utterly convinced that her strongest bond with Jai was sexual rather than emotional. And that awareness stabbed through her in an almost physical pain, she registered then in dismay. Of course, she had kind of known from the start that she wanted more than sex from Jai, but somehow it hadn't crossed her mind that she was *already* much more deeply involved in their relationship than he was.

There was no denying it: she had fallen hopelessly

in love with the man who had married her only to legitimise his son's birth. It had started way back that first night when she had fallen into bed with him and Hari had been conceived in the flare-up of passion between them…and if she was honest with herself, even though she didn't feel she could be *that* honest with Jai, it was an attraction that Jai had *always* held for her.

That long-ago adolescent crush had only been the first indication that she was intensely susceptible to Jai and exposed to him as an adult, the remnants of that crush had simply morphed that first week they were married into something much more powerful. She loved him. That was why she was constantly insecure and prickly and, now, possessive of him. If she hadn't been in love with him, she would have been much less anxious and hurt when he'd chosen to step back from her during the second week they had been together.

And nothing was likely to change, she reflected, deciding to tuck away all her anxiety and bury it, because there was nothing she could do to change either Jai's feelings or her own. It was what it was, and she had to live with it. Certainly, interfering on his mother's behalf, as even his aunt had feared to do, was out of the question.

Even so, she *did* feel that she should meet Lady Milly discreetly and discover the facts for some future date when hopefully she and Jai would have been married long enough for her to trust that they had a stable relationship. After all, it seemed wrong that she, as Jai's wife, should also stand back and do nothing while the poor woman suffered for sins she hadn't committed. It might not be her business in many ways, but Willow had a strong sense of justice. It would do no harm for her to at least listen to the woman while simultaneously introducing her to her grandson, she told herself squarely.

Furthermore, Jai still had the time to mend his relationship with his mother, who clearly loved him. His mother had to love him, for why else would she have fought for years to see him again? Her persistence was self-explanatory. What was more, Milly was family and surely everyone was willing to go that extra mile for a family member? Jai now had a chance that Willow had never had with her own father. She had failed to win her father's love time and time again because really the only thing he had appreciated in a child was the ability to achieve top academic results. But Jai's mother was offering love even after multiple rejections. Unfortunately past hurt and pride would prevent Jai from giving his mother the chance to redeem herself, but what if Willow could take that chance for him and use it?

Cecilia arrived at the Lake Palace for a visit the following afternoon and caught Willow unprepared. She was down on her knees playing with Hari in the nursery with tumbled hair and not a scrap of make-up on when Jai strolled in with Cecilia in tow and not the smallest warning. In that moment, Willow genuinely wanted to kill Jai. She sat up with a feverishly flushed face and struggled to smile politely as Cecilia dropped gracefully down beside her and exclaimed over the resemblance between Hari and Jai.

'He's got your eyes, Jai!' Cecilia crooned in delight, smoothing a hand over Hari's curls. 'He is adorable.'

'Yes, he is,' Willow conceded fondly, stifling her irritation with difficulty.

'Do you remember your father taking us on a tour of the desert that first summer?' Cecilia asked Jai.

And that was the start of the 'do you remember?' game that stretched throughout coffee downstairs as Cecilia encouraged Jai to reminisce about friends from their university days and brought him up to speed on the activities of those he had lost touch with. Willow might as well have been a painting on the wall for all the share she got of the conversation, while Cecilia became more and more animated at the attention she was receiving. It was a total surprise to Willow when Jai smoothly mentioned that they were going out to lunch, an arrangement that was news to her, and moments later Cecilia began making visibly reluctant departure moves.

'So, when was this lunch with Sher arranged?' Willow enquired curiously on the steps of the palace as the blonde was driven off by her driver in an SUV.

'Oh, that's tomorrow,' Jai admitted with a tiny smile of superiority as he absorbed her surprise. 'It was time for Cecilia to leave.'

Disconcerted, Willow turned back to him. 'You mean—?'

'I lied? *Yes*,' Jai interposed with dancing eyes of amusement at her astonishment. 'I will always be polite to Cecilia but I have no wish to socialise with her. Yesterday I was curious, today I was bored with her.'

Relief sank through Willow in a blinding wave. 'But I thought—'

'That I am still naive enough to be duped by a woman who chose to welcome a richer man into her bed?' Jai said, sliding an arm round her slender spine. 'No, I'm not.'

'A richer man?' Willow queried, recalling his aunt's opinion of the beautiful blonde.

'Within a month of breaking off our engagement,

Cecilia was married to the owner of a private bank. Her affair with him began while she was *still* with me,' Jai breathed with sardonic bite. 'Shortly before her change of heart, she had learned that my sole wealth at that point was based on my share of the family trust, and at the time my business was only in its infancy. She went for a more promising option— a much older man with a pile of capital.'

Still frowning, Willow glanced up at him. 'But when it happened you must have been devastated.'

'Not so devastated that I didn't eventually recognise that I'd had a narrow escape,' Jai quipped with raw-edged amusement. 'Her marriage to a man old enough to be her father was the first evidence of her true nature. My mother made the same move,' he extended in a rare casual reference to his parents' marriage. 'Money must've been her main objective too. I can't believe she ever loved my father.'

Willow set her teeth together and said nothing, thinking that his father really had done a number on him, leaving him not one shred of faith in the woman who had brought him into the world and, by achieving that, had ensured that Jai never became curious enough to meet the woman and decide for himself.

Jai came to bed late that night because he had been working. He was a tall sliver of lean, supple beauty in the moonlight, sliding in beside her and reaching for her in almost the same movement.

'You can't,' she told him, feeling awkward because it was that time of the month.

'You mean—?'

'Yes,' she confirmed drowsily.

'Doesn't mean I can't hold you, doesn't mean I can't kiss you,' Jai teased, folding her into his arms regardless. 'This is the very first time I've met with that restriction since my engagement.'

Thinking of all the years he had been free and single, Willow said, 'How can it be?'

'After Cecilia the longest I stayed with a woman was a weekend. It was a practical choice for me, selfish too, I'll admit, but I didn't want anything deeper or more lasting.'

'Oh, dear, and here I am planning to last and last and *last*,' she whispered playfully. 'Maybe you'll eventually love me too because you're stuck with me.'

His lean, strong physique tensed. 'No, the love trail isn't for me. That would be excess, and we don't need it to be happy or raise Hari together. Be practical, *soniyaa*. What we've got is much more realistic.'

A hollow sensation spread inside Willow's chest along with a very strong urge to kick the love of her life out of bed. It was early days, though, she reminded herself, and she was being greedy and impatient. In a year's time she might have grown on him to such an extent that he did love her. Or was that simply a fantasy? If he hadn't been bowled over by her from the outset, she was unlikely ever to become the sole and most important focus of his wants, logic warned her. Unfortunately for her, her heart didn't jump at the words, 'practical' or 'realistic.'

CHAPTER NINE

THEY LUNCHED WITH Sher the following day at his family home, which his late father had allowed to fall into rack and ruin.

Only a small part of the ancient Nizam of Tharistan's palace had so far been made liveable, and they dined in that wing on a shaded terrace overlooking a vast stretch of uncultivated land, which Sher admitted had once been the gardens. At Willow's request he had gathered old records, paintings and photographs from Victorian times in an effort to provide some evidence of what the gardens had once looked like, for what remained was simply undergrowth with the occasional hint of the shape of a path or flowerbed.

'It'll be a massive project,' she warned him. 'And hugely expensive.'

'Not a problem for Sher.' Jai laughed.

'Would it be possible for me to take these records

and old photos home with me?' Willow pressed the other man. 'What you really need is an archaeological garden survey done.'

'No, I'll be content with something in the spirit of the original gardens, rather than requiring an exact replica,' Sher admitted. 'I'll bring the old maps over to you tomorrow. I keep them in a climate-controlled environment but as long as you wear gloves handling them, they'll be fine.'

'I can't wait to see them,' Willow confided, excitement brimming in her sparkling green eyes, all her attention on Sher. 'Of course, I'll wear gloves.'

Lunch with two highly creative people was not to be recommended, Jai decided at that point, unless you were of a similar ilk. And Jai *wasn't*. A garden was only a green space to him that complemented a building. Books, technology and business alone held his interest.

When they had climbed back into the limo, Jai thought he should warn his wife of the possible pitfalls of what she was planning. 'As you said, it will be a huge project,' he reminded her smoothly. 'Do you really know what you're taking on?'

Willow straightened her shoulders and turned to him with an eager smile. 'I can't wait!'

'But it will demand a lot of your time.'

'What else do I have to focus on?' Willow prompted.

Myself and my son, Jai reckoned. But he was too clever to say it out loud, admitting that it sounded like something his elderly father would have said and inwardly wincing at the comparison. 'I had been hoping that you would take on some duties with the foundation when you have the time to decide which of our charitable groups would most interest you,' he commented, and it wasn't a lie, he reasoned, even if that possibility had only just occurred to him. 'It would get you out and about more and give you a role of your own.'

'That's a wonderful suggestion,' Willow said warmly. 'But maybe best saved for when I've fully found my feet here.'

'I thought you already had…found your feet,' he admitted.

'Different country, different culture, different languages, different *everything*,' she enumerated with quiet emphasis. 'I love my life here but right now I'm still acclimatising to the changes. I don't think I'm quite ready yet to step out in a social setting as your Maharani, particularly when everyone will be expecting someone like you, experienced at making speeches and knowledgeable about community work.'

That explanation silenced Jai because he immediately grasped that he had not even considered the changes that her move to India on his behalf had made to her life. Rare discomfiture afflicted him. Had he always been so self-absorbed that he only saw in terms of what best suited him? That disposed to be selfish and arrogant? He gritted his teeth at the suspicion and said no more, quite forgetting the irritation that his best friend had inexplicably evoked in him.

The next morning, Sher brought the maps over and, together, he and Willow pored over the old parchments in the library, Jai soon taking his leave. Searching for evidence of former paths, banks, sunken areas and even small garden buildings, they discovered a wealth of useful facts. Thoroughly enjoying herself, Willow did sketches and made copious notes while Sher talked at length about what he liked to see in a garden. When Jai walked in again, they were trading jokes about what they suspected was the marking for an ancient surprise fountain that had been designed to startle the ladies as they walked past by drenching them.

For a split second, Jai froze on the threshold. Willow and Sher were on a rug on the floor laughing uproariously, one of his friend's hands on her slim shoulder to steady her as she almost overbalanced in her mirth into the welter of papers that surrounded them.

'Lunch,' Jai announced coolly.

'Oh, my goodness, is it *that* time already?' Willow carolled in astonishment, almost as if she hadn't been camping out in the library for a solid four hours with his best friend, Jai thought in disbelief. Evidently when in Sher's company time had wings for his wife.

Sher's entire attention was pinned to Willow's face. His friend was attracted to her. Jai had already guessed that, for Willow was a classic beauty, but then Sher was attracted to a lot of women and, as a former Bollywood star, he flirted with *all* of them, be they grandmothers or teenagers, because he was accustomed to playing to admiring crowds. Even so, Jai trusted Sher with his wife, *totally* trusted him. He was fully aware that his friend would never *ever* cross a line with a married woman because that same scenario had destroyed Sher's parents' marriage.

No, Jai didn't blame Sher for the intimate scene he had interrupted, he blamed Willow for getting too friendly, for curling up on the floor and making herself recklessly, dangerously approachable, *his* Maharani, acting like a giggly, frisky schoolgirl, he thought furiously. A man less sophisticated than Sher might have read her signals wrong and taken advantage, might have *made a move* on her, the concept of which sent such a current of lancing rage shooting through Jai that he clenched his lean hands into angry fists of restraint by his sides.

He wouldn't lose his temper when he spoke to Willow later, but he would give her useful advice on how to keep other men at a safe distance, advice she certainly needed if what he was seeing was likely to be typical of her behaviour in male company.

'You've been very quiet,' Willow commented over dinner, hours after Sher had departed, leaving her free to spend a contented afternoon pondering the old photos while trying to visualise the lush and colourful garden that Sher would most enjoy.

That was the moment that Jai became aware that what he had *planned* to say to his wife didn't sound quite the same as when he had first thought the matter over. He breathed in deep and decided that tact was all very well, but it might not get across the exact message he wanted to impart and that message was too important to hold back.

'You flirt with Sher and I dislike it,' Jai delivered bluntly, pushing back his chair and rising from his seat with his wine glass elegantly cupped in one lean brown hand.

For the count of ten seconds, Willow simply gaped at him in disbelief. *He did not just say that, he could not have accused me of* that, she was thinking, and then she looked at him, really looked at his lean, darkly handsome face, and realised by the glitter of his ice-blue eyes and the taut line of his sensual mouth that, no, sadly, he hadn't been joking. She was stunned, incredulous that he could have misunder- stood her banter with Sher to that extent, and then just as quickly angry at the speed with which he had misjudged her. In turn, she too rose from her chair and left the table.

'For goodness' sake, I don't flirt with Sher,' she said defensively. 'It's only a friendly thing, nothing the slightest bit suspect about it. I don't know how you could possibly think otherwise.'

Jai's cool appraisal didn't waver. 'But I do. You need to learn how to keep a certain distance in your manner with other men.'

'And you need to learn how not to be irrationally jealous!' Willow slammed back at him without warn- ing, her patience tested beyond its limits and flam- ing into throbbing resentment.

Those two words, 'irrational' and 'jealous,' struck Jai like bricks. He didn't do either emotion. Unfortu- nately, those same words also hooked into a phrase his aunt had, many years earlier, once used to de- scribe his father. Later, when challenged by Jai, Jivika had withdrawn the comment and, unfortu- nately, Willow's use of those offensive words sent a wave of antipathy travelling through him. 'I'm not jealous, Willow. I'm merely asking you to monitor your behaviour in male company.'

'But you'd really prefer me *not* to have male friends?' Willow darted back at him.

Disconcerted by that surprising question, Jai frowned. 'Well, yes, that may be the wisest approach.'

'So, quite obviously, you *are* the jealous, possessive, irrational type you think you aren't…or possibly a throwback to the dinosaurs when men and women didn't make friends with the opposite sex?' Willow shot back at him wrathfully. 'Obviously you have about as much self-awareness as a stone in the wall! Sher's like the brother I never had!'

'You don't have a brother!' Jai fired back at her.

'Didn't I just say that?' Willow exclaimed furiously. 'There was no flirting between us, nothing anyone could criticise. I like him and that's *it*! I certainly don't fancy him.'

Marginally mollified by that admission and aware that Ranjit was loitering in the dining room beyond the doors opening out onto the terrace, Jai murmured in an effort to lower the volume of their dispute, 'I'm not even saying that you knew that you were flirting. It may have been quite unconscious on your part.'

'Well, it must have been unconscious because I don't think I even know *how* to flirt, with my lack of experience in that field!' Willow slung back at him even louder. 'Whatever you think you *saw* between Sher and me, you got it wrong, Jai.'

The doors eased shut with diplomatic quietness and colour edged Jai's spectacular cheekbones. She was being unreasonable, and he didn't know how what he had said had escalated into a full-blown acrimonious scene. He was not the jealous type and he was never, ever irrational and, had he been possessive, he would have stopped Sher from offering her the project in the first instance. And now, he wished he *had* done that, he conceded grimly.

'I didn't get it wrong,' he insisted, refusing to yield an inch.

Willow lifted her chin, outraged green eyes locking to his. 'You got it wrong in every way possible,' she told him succinctly. 'There was no flirting but if you can't even admit that you're jealous, how is anyone to persuade you that you're wrong? All right, I'll even make it easier for you. I'll admit that initially I was jealous of Cecilia.'

'Why on earth would you be jealous of *her*?' Jai demanded in astonishment.

'Because she was all over you like a rash at the party and at no time did I see *you* pushing her away and respecting the sort of boundaries you're accusing me of breaking with Sher!' Willow accused.

'That was a different situation,' Jai argued. 'She

was a friend long before I became more deeply involved with her.'

'Oh, have it your own way!' Willow snapped back in frustration, wishing she could get inside his head to rearrange his brain into a pattern she could recognise. 'I'm done here. I've got nothing more to say to you until you admit that you're a jealous, possessive toad, and then I *might* forgive you for insulting me!'

Beneath Jai's speechless gaze, Willow rammed open the door and vanished back into the palace without another word. He refilled his wine glass and stood looking out over the lake, watching a sloth bear slurp a noisy drink at the edge of the lake while the chitter chatter of monkeys at dusk filled the air. Slowly he breathed in deeply, telling himself he had been foolish to assume that marriage would be an easy ride.

And yet it generally *was* with Willow, he conceded grudgingly. She had slotted into his life as though she had always been there, and he shared more with her than he had ever shared with a woman. At the outset, he had assumed that their marriage would be all about Hari, only it wasn't. Their son was a point of connection, but it was Willow's unspoilt, gentle nature, her lack of feminine guile and her interest in learning about everything that was new to her that continued to intrigue Jai. The flirting, most probably, had been unconscious, he decided, and possibly he should have kept his reservations about the degree of friendliness between his wife and his best friend to himself.

After all, he fully trusted Sher, so why hadn't he had the same amount of faith in Willow? Hadn't he once even cherished the insane suspicion that Willow might have been a fortune hunter? Was he so truly a prisoner of his father's unhappy past and Cecilia's mercenary betrayal that he could not trust a woman? That idea shook him and put him into a brooding mood before he went back to his office to work, as was his wont, to escape his uneasy thoughts.

Several hours later, he entered their bedroom quietly and discovered the ultimate bed-blocker blinking up at him in the moonlight: his son, snuggled up next to his mother. Hari closed his eyes again and Jai went off to find another bed.

Willow woke early the next morning with Hari tugging at her hair, and looked down at her son in surprise because she hadn't intended him to spend the night with her, had simply fallen asleep while cuddling him for comfort. It's not safe to sleep with him, her conscience reproached her, and she freshened up and returned Hari to the nursery staff, who greeted him as though he had been absent a week. She breakfasted alone, assuming Jai was already in his office because he was fond of dawn starts. Her annoyance with him was still intense, but she was troubled by the stand-off she had initiated the night before because Jai could be as stubborn and unyielding as the rock she had compared him to.

Willow sighed. She had had to confront him. He had not given her a choice and how could she compromise? The answer was that on such a dangerous point of contention, she *couldn't* compromise, not if she wanted their relationship to have a future. That truth acknowledged, she frowned as she realised that this was also the morning Jai's mother had invited her to meet her. She hadn't had time to dwell on that thorny issue in recent days but now it was first and foremost in her mind.

Did she ignore that invitation as Jai would unquestionably expect her to do, or did she meet Lady Milly because she now knew, thanks to Jivika, that Jai's mother had been cruelly misjudged?

Surely she had a right to discover the facts of the situation for herself? Or, even as Jai's wife, was that background none of her business? Sadly, Jai was too loyal to his father's memory to take advantage of the same opportunity, she reflected, and that was tragic. Maybe she could be a peacemaker, a go-between, she thought optimistically. If the meeting went the right way, it could bring Jai a great deal of happiness, she

reasoned, her heart lifting at that optimistic prospect. Even Jai's aunt, however, had been unwilling
to run the risk of getting involved and yet Jivika was
neither a weak nor timid personality. Willow's teeth
worried anxiously at her lower lip as she weighed
the odds and then a rueful smile slowly crept across
her lips because when it got down to basics, it was
a simple decision.

Jai had been badly damaged and hurt by his conviction that his mother had abandoned him as a baby.
Willow loved him, even when she was angry with
him. If there was anything she could do to ease that
pain that Jai fought to hide from the world, she *would*
do it. And if he rediscovered a lost mother from the
exercise, it would be well worth the risk she took and
far more than she had ever managed to achieve with
her own father, she conceded sadly.

A couple of hours later, Willow walked into the
Royal Chandrapur, an exclusive boutique establish-
ment on the other side of the city. From reception, she
wheeled Hari's buggy into the tiny lift and breathed
in deep.

The first surprise was that the small blond woman
who opened the door to her appeared to be much
younger than she had expected. Well-preserved, she
assumed, meeting eyes of the same startling pale

blue as her husband's and taking in the huge smile on the other woman's face.

'I didn't think you'd come,' she said frankly.

Willow winced. 'I almost didn't. Jai doesn't know I'm here,' she admitted guiltily.

'And this is…little Hari?'

As the door closed behind them, Jai's mother knelt down by the side of the buggy and studied Willow's son in fascination. 'He is spookily like Jai was at the same age,' she whispered appreciatively. 'Just a little older than Jai was when I left India.'

Willow breathed in deep and settled into the seat the other woman indicated with a casual hand. 'What I don't understand is, if you wanted contact with Jai why did you virtually cut him dead when you did finally meet him as an adult?'

'Let me start at the beginning and then perhaps you'll understand better. If you don't, that's fine too. I'm grateful you came here. First of all, I am Milly… and you are… Willow, I gather?'

Willow harnessed the very rude impatience tugging at her and nodded with a smile.

'Would you like tea?'

'No, thanks. Being here with you makes me a little nervous. Let's talk about whatever we have to talk about,' Willow urged.

'A little background first, then,' Milly decided,

seemingly magnetised by the tiny fingers Hari was stretching out to her. 'May I lift him?' she asked hopefully.

Leaning down, Willow detached the harness and watched her son being scooped gently into his grandmother's arms.

'Where do I start?' Milly sighed then. 'I was twenty and Jai's father was fifty when we married. My family were against it from the start because of the age gap but I was madly in love and I thought I knew it all.'

'I didn't know that there was such a big age gap between you,' Willow admitted.

'The marriage didn't work from the start. Rehan wanted a quiet little wife, who stayed at home, and I was very independent. He was insanely jealous and controlling but the assaults didn't begin until after Jai was born,' Milly murmured flatly.

Willow's clear gaze widened in dismay. 'He *hit* you?' she exclaimed.

Milly nodded. 'We had terrible rows and he couldn't control his temper. But I'm talking about slaps and kicks, not severe beatings.'

'Abuse is abuse,' Willow opined.

'When my mother was dying, I had to return to England to be with her and, before I left, I made the mistake of telling Rehan that I believed we should separate. My biggest mistake, though, was agree-ing to leave Jai behind until I came back. I was only away for two weeks,' Milly proffered. 'Rehan at-tended my mother's funeral and brought what he said were divorce papers for me to sign but they were all in Hindi. I was so relieved that he was willing to let me go without a fuss that I signed… I hadn't the smallest suspicion that I was surrendering my right to have custody of my son or access to him and by the time I realised that it was too late.'

'Jai's father tricked you?' Willow was appalled.

Milly lifted a thick file on the small table be-tween them and extended it. 'If you can do nothing else, give this to Jai. It's the proof of all the years I fought through the courts to try and regain access to him. I failed.'

'But why, if you *wanted* to see him, did you deny him or whatever it was you did when you *did* see him?' Willow demanded bluntly.

'My husband and stepchildren didn't know Jai ex-isted at that stage,' Milly volunteered shamefacedly. 'Steven, my second husband, knew about my mar-riage to Rehan but I didn't tell him that I'd had a child. My battle to see Jai consumed a decade and a half of my life and I got nowhere in all that time. I needed to move on to retain my sanity and make a fresh start. But I *will* admit that I was fearful of telling Steven that I had been deprived of my right to see my own child because, with three kids of his own, it might have made him doubt the wisdom of marrying me.'

The picture Willow was forming became a little clearer in receipt of that frank admission. 'Steven had three children? They're not yours?' she prompted.

'He was a widower with a young family when we met. I did hope to have another child, but I was almost forty by the time we married and it didn't happen. It was only a few months afterwards that I ran into Jai in the flesh,' his mother confided with tears in her eyes. 'Someone actually introduced me to him... I was floored—there he was in front of me with his face stiffening as he realised who I was and I had been too scared to tell Steven about him! I walked away because I didn't know what else to do with other people all around us. I wasn't prepared.'

'And then you tried to see Jai afterwards to explain,' Willow filled in with a grimace. 'And it was too late. The damage was done.'

Milly's regret was palpable as she rocked Hari, who was curled up in her arms, perfectly content. 'If only people stayed this innocent.' She sighed. 'I left a baby behind and now he's a man and they're much more complicated.'

Tell me about it, Willow ruminated uneasily, won-

dering whether she should go straight back to the
Lake Palace and tell Jai who she had been with, or
whether to go shopping instead in an effort to make
her cover-up lie the truth, which would give her time
to choose the optimum moment for such a revelation.
But would there ever be a right moment to tackle so
very personal and controversial a subject?

Deepening the deception she was already engaged
in, however, felt even more wrong to her. Indeed,
even being with Milly without her son's knowledge
felt wrong to Willow at that moment. But good intentions had to count for something, didn't they?
She argued with herself as she lifted the file and
told Milly that she needed to get home but hoped to
see her again. The older woman's answering smile
was sad, as if she seriously doubted the likelihood of
them ever having a second meeting, and she thanked
Willow heartily again for being willing to see her and
giving her the chance to meet her grandson. When
Willow mentioned Jivika's input, Milly simply rolled
her eyes, unimpressed.

'Jivika is sincere,' Willow insisted defensively.

'But nothing's changed. My ex-husband and, by
the sound of it, now Jai as well have too much influence, too much status to be treated like ordinary people.' Milly studied her with embittered eyes. 'They
may not rule any more but they're still royal in the

eyes of thousands. That's why I never had a hope of fighting Rehan and winning. It was never an equal playing field. There were witnesses, who could've supported me but who were unwilling to expose their Maharaja for the man he really was.'

'I'm truly sorry,' Willow muttered uncomfortably. 'I can't promise anything, but I will *try* to talk to Jai some time soon.'

Even if it cost her *her* marriage? she asked herself worriedly as the limo drove back to the palace with Hari dozing contentedly in his child seat. Or was that an exaggerated fear? Who could tell how badly Jai would react? No, it wasn't her place to act as a persuader, she reasoned uneasily. She would admit to meeting up with his mother and give him the file and leave it at that. She had interfered enough. He would make up his own mind about what, if anything, he wanted to do with what he learned.

When Jai went in search of Willow mid-morning he assumed she had gone to see Sher until he recalled that his friend had mentioned a trip to Mumbai that day, and he phoned her driver instead to discover where she had gone. A hotel? A moment later he rang the hotel and without hesitation requested a list of the British guests staying there. Only a few minutes beyond that he knew the only possible reason for his wife's visit to the Royal Chandrapur and he could not credit that, after what he had told her, she could have gone to meet his mother. It outraged him and it didn't make sense to him. Even so, by the time acceptance of that unwelcome fact had set in, his outrage had settled into a far more dangerous sense of betrayal.

When Willow climbed out of the limo carrying her sleeping son, eager hands were extended to take him back to the nursery and his lunch. Straightening, she headed up the shallow marble steps and saw Jai poised in the empty hall. One glance at the narrowed chilling glitter of his eyes and the forbidding coolness of his lean, strong features and her stomach dropped as though the ground beneath her feet had suddenly vanished. Her mouth ran dry and she swallowed painfully.

CHAPTER TEN

'You know where I've been,' Willow guessed, her fingers biting into the heavy file she clasped in one hand. 'Let me explain.'

'Let me make it clear from the start—there *is* no acceptable explanation,' Jai asserted, his shadowed, well-defined jaw line clenching hard as he strode into the library.

He leant back against the desk in the centre of the room, tall and lean and bronzed and beautiful, and her heart clenched because there was a look in his eyes that she had never seen before and it frightened her. He looked detached, wholly in control and calm but utterly distant, as if she were a stranger.

'How did my mother contact you?' Jai shot the question at her.

'By email. One of your staff gave it to me.' Willow shrugged awkwardly. 'I suppose they didn't want to give it to you. I wasn't even going to mention it to you after what you'd told me about her, but then I had a conversation with…er…someone at the party that made me realise that there are two sides to every story.'

Jai elevated an eloquent black brow. *'Someone?'*

Stiff as a board, Willow angled an uneasy hand in dismissal. 'I'm not going to name names. I don't want you dragging anyone else into this mess. I don't want you to be angry with anyone but me.'

'I'm not angry. I am stunned by your intrusion into a matter that is confidential. But I am repelled by what can only be your insatiable curiosity and your complete lack of sensitivity!' Jai enumerated in a voice that shook slightly, belying his contention that he was not angry.

Willow's tummy turned over sickly and her natural colour ebbed. 'I intended to tell you.'

'But you still went to see her,' Jai condemned harshly. 'You knew how I would feel about that and yet *still* you went to see her—to do *what*? To discuss long-past events that are none of your business? To listen to her lies?'

'It's not rational for you to place a complete block on her side of the story or to assume that she's lying without hearing the facts,' Willow dared, but then fear of the trouble she had already caused between them punctured her bravado. 'But I *am* very sorry that I've upset you.'

Jai raked long brown fingers through his luxuriant black hair. 'You let me down. You deceived me.'

'I didn't deceive you!' she gasped in dismay.

'Not telling me that you were planning to meet her was a deception, an unforgivable deception!' Jai ground out in a raw undertone. 'You quite deliberately went behind my back to do something which you knew went against my principles.'

'But I had good intentions,' Willow muttered frantically, her chest tightening at the bite of that threatening word, 'unforgivable,' being attached to anything she had done. 'Feelings always win out over principles with me.'

'I trusted you.'

'No, you've never trusted me. You don't even trust me with your best friend,' Willow reminded him helplessly.

A tinge of dark colour edged Jai's high cheekbones and he studied her grimly. 'I got over that. I worked it out for myself. I *was* jealous of the bond you seem to have forged with Sher and it unsettled me,' he admitted flatly. 'I wasn't thinking logically when I spoke to you yesterday and the issue would've been cleared up last night had you not taken Hari to bed with you. I didn't want to disturb you.'

'You mean...you came to see me later on?' Willow prompted in surprise.

Jai jerked his arrogant dark head in confirmation.

'Thank you for that,' Willow acknowledged tautly, conceding that at least that issue now seemed to have been laid to rest, but not comforted by that knowledge when a bigger abyss seemed to have opened up between them. A gulf she was wholly responsible for creating, she conceded wretchedly.

And she wasn't surprised by that, not now, when she could see the very real damage that she had done with her foolish attempt at undercover sleuthing on his behalf. Jai still emanated tension and the raw glitter of his pale eyes and the compression of his lips remained unchanged. He was convinced that she had betrayed his trust. She had hurt him, and she hadn't meant to, but that wasn't much consolation for her at that moment. Hurting Jai when she had intended only to help him was a real slap in the face.

But then what had she thought she could possibly accomplish when the subject of his estranged mother was still so raw with him that he didn't even like to discuss it? Trying to play God usually got people into trouble, she reflected unhappily. Her handling of the issue had been downright clumsy and poorly thought through. Her hand ached with the tight grip she still had on the file in her hand and she settled it down heavily on the desk.

'Your mother gave this to me.'

'I don't want it…whatever it is,' Jai bit out.

'It's a record of all the legal action she took while you were still a child when she was fighting to gain access to you. Solicitor's letters, family court decisions. It's all there in black and white. I can explain why she couldn't face speaking to you in public as well.'

'I'm not interested.'

'Well, that's your decision,' Willow agreed tightly. 'But if you want my opinion—'

'I *don't*,' Jai sliced in curtly as he swept up the file in one powerful hand. 'I will ensure that this is returned to her.'

'All right.' Willow raised her hands in a semi-soothing gesture as she stepped back from the desk. 'I won't say any more. I may have blundered in where angels fear to tread but I didn't mean to cause this much trouble or harm anyone.'

Jai stared at her with unnerving intensity. 'Why *did* you do it?'

Willow could feel the blood in her face draining away with the stress of that simple acerbic question. 'I thought I could help. I suppose that was pretty naive of me.'

'*Who* did you wish to help?' Jai demanded in a savage undertone of condemnation. 'I'm a grown man, Willow. My father is dead, and I grew up without a mother. I didn't miss my mother because I never knew her. I am more concerned by the damage you have done to us.'

'Us?' she repeated uncertainly.

His lean, darkly handsome features hardened, his eyes chilling to polar ice. 'How do you think that we—our marriage—can possibly come back from this betrayal?' he slung at her rawly.

Willow stared back at him in shock at that stinging question. Was he saying that he truly could not forgive her for what she had done? Perspiration broke out on her brow. Suddenly she felt sick, shaky with fear.

Jai paced angrily away from her as though he could not bear to be too close to her. 'You keep secrets from me,' he condemned harshly, his distaste unhidden. 'You kept your pregnancy and the birth of my son a secret. You kept my mother's email a secret and you intended to keep your visit to her a secret as well for who knows how long!'

'Only because I wanted to meet her and give her a chance!' Willow argued in desperation.

'You said I lacked trust and understanding but have you considered your own flaws?' Jai asked with cruel clarity. 'What do I care about a woman who walked away from me thirty years ago? You and Hari are supposed to be my family now *and* the only family I need. But when I look at the deceit and disloyalty you are capable of, I feel like a fool and I cannot see a future for us!'

Frozen to the beautiful Persian rug, Willow watched Jai walk back out of the library again while her heart plummeted to basement level. Shattered, she just stood there. If he couldn't see a future for them, where did that leave her? Did that mean he was thinking about a divorce? *Truly?* Was their marriage over now because she had angered and disappointed him? But Jai believed that she had betrayed him and that went *deep*.

When she walked through the hall, Ranjit reminded her that lunch was ready. Although she had absolutely no appetite, she struggled to behave normally, to behave as though her life hadn't just fallen apart in front of her, and she headed out to the coolness of the terrace with a heavy heart, praying that Jai would join her and give her the chance to reason with him.

There, however, she sat in solitary splendour, striving to act as though nothing had happened while pushing food round her plate. She had messed up. Correction, she had messed up spectacularly. Jai had moved on from his dysfunctional beginnings. He might still be sensitive about his mother's apparent desertion, but he had learned to live with it, and he hadn't needed her stirring up those muddy waters again.

More tellingly, Jai was much more disturbed by the truth that she had kept secrets from him and acted without his knowledge. Her heart sank because she *was* guilty of making those mistakes and had little defence to offer on that score.

She hadn't known Jai when she'd conceived a child with him. She hadn't known how straight and blunt and honest he was or how much he valued those traits. Loving him, however, she had blundered in, convinced she could act as a peacemaker between him and his estranged mother. How on earth had she been so stupid that she had gone digging into his past, believing that she could somehow heal old wounds and make him happy? Nothing was ever that simple and adults were much more multifaceted than children. As he had reminded her, he was an adult now with a different outlook and values and he was infinitely more disturbed by the reality that the wife he had just begun to trust had let him down than by old history.

Jai had looked at her and found her wanting, Willow registered sickly. Her own father had always looked at her in that light, as his disappointing daughter, who had failed to live up to his fond hopes for her. Being a disappointment was nothing new to Willow but, when the judge was Jai, her failure to reach his standards cut through every layer of skin and hurt as fiercely as an acid burn. Distressed, she left the table to go and find Jai again and attempt to explain the motivation behind her interference.

He wasn't in his office and she wandered through the beautiful rooms until she found him in the relatively small room that his father had used as a study. Above the desk hung a handsome portrait of his late father, Rehan, in a traditional Rajput warrior pose. Jai was in an armchair, his lean, lithe body sleek and taut in an innately graceful sprawl. He had a whiskey glass in his hand and a reckless glitter lit up his bright gaze. Willow's eyes zoomed straight to the file that lay open on the desktop.

'I need to explain things,' she murmured tautly. 'You have to understand why I did what I did…'

'What's to explain?' Jai asked flatly, his wide sensual mouth settling into a grim line. 'There is no arguing with what's contained in that file. Obviously, the father I idolised lied to me all my life and behind those lies there *must* be even worse revelations. People with nothing to hide don't lie.'

'Jai… I—'

'The someone who tipped you off could only have been my aunt, Jivika,' Jai guessed, rising abruptly from his seat. 'Jivika will know everything and that's who I need to speak to now and finish this.'

Willow froze on the threshold of the room, recognising the pain darkening his eyes and shrinking from it in the knowledge that she had inflicted it on him by forcing him to deal with painful truths. 'Let the dust settle first. Mull it over. And don't forget,' she muttered ruefully, 'we all have a good side and a bad side. No matter what you find out one fact doesn't change—you still had a wonderful father who loved you.'

'Who told me that my mother was the love of his life…and yet, according to those documents, he abused her,' Jai breathed with a shudder of revulsion, his shame at such a revelation palpable. 'He lied on so many different levels that are unpardonable. Jivika, however, will know everything and she's family. It will be confidential. I have to know it *all* now.'

For the first time, Willow understood why Jai's aunt had resisted the temptation to interfere, because the ugly truth about his parents' marriage had devastated Jai, rolling a wrecking ball through his every conviction and fond memory. 'I was so naive about this situation,' she confided with heartfelt regret. 'I thought I could fix things but all I've done is cause more damage.'

'No,' Jai contradicted squarely, springing upright and towering over her. 'Even the toughest truths shouldn't be concealed from those concerned.'

'Even when you consider what it's done to our relationship?' she pressed unhappily.

'You were trying to right an injustice. I can respect that,' Jai told her tightly. 'But I don't know if I can accept it and still live with you.'

His savage honesty crushed her. It contained none of the emotion she had longed to see coming in her direction. As Jai left the palace to visit his aunt, her tummy gave a nauseous flip and she turned away again, reckoning that whatever he learned would only cause him more distress. Ultimately, Jai *could* forgive her because she had exposed a truth that should never have been hidden from him, but it didn't mean he would like her for it or that he would want to continue their marriage with a woman he didn't feel he could trust. Nor was he likely to love her for shining a bright light over his father's deceit and his mother's victimhood. And love was what she was always seeking from Jai and least likely to receive, because love had much more humble beginnings.

Sometimes she thought that she had fallen in love with Jai the first time he smiled at her. Or had it hap-

pened when he wrapped an arm round her and of-
fered her comfort, showing her a level of tenderness
and understanding that she had never experienced
before? Yet, it had been his raw, uninhibited passion
that had exploded her out of the almost dreamlike
state in which she had then lived her life, humbly
accepting her limitations while doggedly following
her own path and striving to rise above her father's
dissatisfaction with her. In matters of the heart, however, she had been naive until Jai came back into
her life. Back then she had kept safe within narrow guidelines, never taking a risk, never allowing
herself to want anything that seemed as if it might
be out of reach. Jai, however, had been a huge risk,
and marrying a man so far removed from her in
terms of looks, status and wealth had been a challenge because right from the start she had felt out
of her depth.

And now she was drowning in a deep sense of loss
because she knew that Jai would never look at her
in the same way again. Whatever she had achieved,
whatever wrong she had tried to put right, she had
been disloyal to him and once again she had acted
behind his back, employing the secrecy that he ab-
horred. A prey to her tumultuous emotions, Willow
found it impossible to settle to any task while Jai
was still out.

Mid-afternoon, she heard the musicians strike up and watched Ranjit make a beeline for the entrance before forcing herself to walk upstairs and take refuge in their bedroom. If he wanted to discuss anything with her, he could come and find her. In the short-term it would be tactless of her to intrude when he probably still needed time and space to absorb what he had learned. Fed up with the warring thoughts assailing her and the almost overwhelming desire to run to his side and offer comfort, she kicked off her shoes and lay down on the bed, fighting her own inclinations to leave him alone rather than crowd him. After all, if she crowded him, she might only encourage him to dwell on the negative feelings he had been having about their marriage before his departure.

When Jai strode through the bedroom door and gave her a brilliant shimmering smile, it utterly disconcerted her. In consternation, Willow sat up and stared at him.

'After what I said to you in my state of shock, I'm surprised that you're still here,' Jai admitted tautly, 'and not on the first flight back to London.'

'Some of what you said was fair. I *did* keep secrets, but only because I didn't want to upset you. I honestly believed that telling you I was pregnant would be the worst news you'd ever heard,' Willow confided ruefully. 'And I couldn't face it.'

'After you, Hari's the best thing that ever happened to me,' Jai murmured in confident rebuttal. 'I didn't appreciate that when I first found out about him. But he gave us the chance to be together in a way that I could cope with.'

Her smooth brow furrowed because she didn't understand. She had expected Jai to return angry or despondent, but he was demonstrating neither reaction. 'Cope with?' she queried.

'I've never been into relationships. I've avoided normal relationships as if they were toxic,' he reminded her uncomfortably. 'My father never recovered from losing my mother and I was always very aware of that. It made me very reluctant to get in too deep with a woman and, when I did break that rule, I ended up with Cecilia and that was a hard lesson too. I didn't have another relationship until I met you and that's why it's been rocky between us and I've been…' his shrug was uneasy '…all over the place with you.'

'All over the place?' she repeated uncertainly.

'When I married you I assumed we would have a detached marriage where after a while we each operated separately, but it didn't turn out like that and I found the closeness that seemed so natural between us…well, for me it was primarily unnerving. I hadn't bargained on feeling that way and I backed off fast,' he extended ruefully.

Recalling the second week of their marriage, Willow released a sigh. 'That hurt me.'

A wry smile slashed the tension from Jai's beautifully modelled mouth. 'And you called me on it, which was typical of you. I wasn't used to that either. Women have always treated me as though everything I do is right and amazing…and then *you* came along.'

Willow winced. 'Yes, and then I came along,' she echoed unhappily.

'And you challenged me every step of the way. You insisted that I treated you with respect. You had your opinions and your own way of looking at things and, while you were happy to listen to my viewpoint, you were independent, and I've never met with that before in a woman. You disagree with me. You were different and I liked that,' he admitted tautly. 'It's a remarkably attractive talent, frustrating too, but I've discovered that I find it much more stimulating than having my ego stroked.'

Willow breathed in deep, wondering where the conversation was heading. 'Really? Well, that's fortunate because I think you have a very healthy ego as it is. You'd become unbearable if I agreed with everything you said.'

Jai laughed softly. 'Probably, but not while you're around,' he acknowledged. 'I haven't been a mega success at being a husband, have I?' He shifted an expressive brown hand and groaned. 'You get to me on levels I never expected to visit with a woman. It throws me off balance and then I get all worked up and I overreact like I did last night when I accused you of flirting with Sher…and as I did today.'

Willow nodded slowly. 'I hope you now realise that's there's nothing—'

'I was jealous,' Jai framed with grim finality. 'Jealous for the first time ever, so *that* meant the fault had to be yours, not mine. I didn't want to *talk* about it last night. I wanted to slide into bed with you and whisper, "I'm a jealous toad," and drown my hurt pride in sex, but you had Hari with you and I didn't want to disturb the two of you. I bet Hari would have started crying if you tried to return him to his lonely cot.'

Her natural smile drove what remained of her tension from her heart-shaped face. 'Oh, dear…' she whispered, and she extended a forgiving hand to him. 'You should've woken me. I wouldn't have minded. I didn't mean to fall asleep with Hari. I was sort of using him like a teddy bear for comfort.'

'I'd much rather you used me for comfort,' Jai confided, closing his hand over hers and using that connection to tug her off the side of the bed and into his arms. He covered her mouth slowly and urgently with his and kissed her breathless. She leant against him for support, letting the remainder of her tension drain away.

'I went to see your mother because—' she began awkwardly.

'No, not now,' Jai interrupted, pressing a fingertip against her parted lips. 'Let tonight be for us. Anyway, I'm reasonably intelligent. I've already worked out *why* you did it.'

'Have you really?' she asked.

'Yes,' Jai assured her with satisfaction. 'I'm getting better at understanding how your mind works. Jivika dropped you in it. Her knowledge has been burning a hole in her brain for years and she jumped at the chance to share. And, you being you, you couldn't resist the urge to try and create a happy ending for everyone involved.'

'Principally you,' Willow whispered. 'It was arrogant of me to think I knew best.'

'And even more arrogant of me to start ranting about disloyalty and deception because the woman I know and love isn't capable of that kind of betrayal,' he concluded.

Willow froze. 'Know...and *love*?'

'Passionately love,' Jai qualified levelly. 'I love

you in a way I have never loved any woman and I didn't even realise it was love. I told myself all sorts of face-saving lies when I stopped having sex with other women after that night I spent with you.'

Her gaze flew up to his in shock. 'Are you saying that you weren't with anyone else after me…all those months?' she prompted in disbelief.

'Yes. I persuaded myself that my celibacy was down to guilt at having taken advantage of you. I even assumed that I'd somehow gone off sex. When I tried repeatedly to check up on you afterwards, I told myself it was because I felt responsible for your well-being. In fact, what I was feeling was really quite simple, I just wanted to *see* you again, but I wasn't ready to admit that to myself.'

Willow, however, was still in shock and concentrating on only one startling fact at a time. 'You mean all that time while I was pregnant and raising Hari you didn't—'

'I haven't been with anyone else since our first night,' Jai confirmed. 'I didn't *want* anyone else. What I found with you was so good that every other experience paled in comparison. So, yes, I was in love with you from way back then and, no, I didn't understand that.'

Willow's eyes rounded in wonder and she looked up into those gorgeous arctic-blue eyes and suddenly she was smiling. 'I love you too,' she told him quietly and without fanfare.

'I was hoping so,' Jai admitted, smiling down at her with love and tenderness gleaming in his intent gaze. 'I mean, you had the bravery to confront me with something everyone else ran scared from, and I very much hoped that love gave you the strength to go against my wishes in the belief that what you found out might make me happier.'

'You understand,' she breathed in relief.

'Of course I do. In the equivalent position I would have done the same thing for you. I very much regret that I wasn't around when your father was doing a number on your self-confidence,' he confessed. 'It also made me appreciate that he had a side to his character that I never saw, a less presentable side.'

'I'm sorry about what you've had to hear about your father.'

'Later, not now,' he insisted again, brushing her hair back from her cheeks and reaching behind her to run the zip down on her dress. 'Tonight is all about us and I'm determined that nothing will come between us.'

'Literally!' She gasped as her dress pooled round her feet and he dispensed with her bra even faster.

Jai skimmed off her panties and lifted her back onto the bed, standing back from her to strip off his clothes with near indecent haste. 'I'm burning for you,' he groaned.

He came down to her, his skin on hers feverishly hot and his sensual mouth hungry and urgent, both hands holding hers to the mattress until they fought free to sink into his luxuriant hair. In the space of minutes her life had been transformed by the simple truth that the man she loved not only understood her, but also loved her back with all the fierce emotion she had long craved. Happiness flooded her like a rejuvenating force, every insecurity forced out and forgotten because what she had most wanted in the world had suddenly become hers.

'I'm crazy about you,' Jai husked in the aftermath of their unashamed passion. 'I couldn't wait to get back here to be with you because I so much regretted what I'd said to you and nothing else mattered. The past is the past and I don't want to revisit it, now that the truth is out.'

'Meaning?' she prompted.

'There will be no recriminations. Not on my part. We all get a clean sheet. My father's behaviour almost destroyed my mother and the guilt of knowing that and remaining silent tormented Jivika for years. We'll leave all that behind us now and my mother will be part of our lives,' he outlined.

'You've *seen* your mother? You've spoken to her?'

'Yes, but only very briefly,' Jai told her with a rueful smile as he looked down at her, his lean, darkly handsome face pensive. 'Unfortunately, she's flying back to London tomorrow and it's her stepdaughter's wedding in a couple of days, so she couldn't delay her flight. But she's planning to come back for a visit in a few weeks and spend time with us.'

'She must've been shocked when you showed up at the hotel,' Willow remarked.

'Shocked, delighted, tearful. We have a lot to catch up on, but we'll take our time,' Jai murmured, curving an arm round Willow to press her closer. 'And if it wasn't for you I wouldn't even have had the opportunity to meet her and give her that chance. For that I owe you a debt I can never repay.'

'Oh, I'll take it out of your hide somehow,' Willow teased, running an appreciative hand down over a long, lean, hair-dusted thigh. 'Don't you worry about that. You'll be paying it off for a very long time and, I promise you now, it's likely to use up every ounce of your surplus energy.'

Jai burst out laughing and crushed her lips under his. 'I love you so much, *balmaa*.'

Willow succumbed to a shameless little wriggle of encouragement and pressed her mouth tenderly to a bare brown shoulder. 'I love you too and I'm going to have to learn Hindi to know what you're calling me.'

'Beloved,' Jai translated, a little breathless as her wandering hands stroked across the taut expanse of his flat stomach.

'I like that,' she told him happily. 'I like that very much indeed.'

EPILOGUE

IN AN ELEGANT shift dress the shade of polished copper, Willow studied her reflection in the mirror. The dress was very flattering, the ultimate in maternity wear, and very nearly concealed the bump of her second pregnancy.

A pair of lean bronzed hands settled gently on her hips from behind and she grinned as Jai's hands slowly slid round to caress her swollen stomach. She adored the fact that he was so ridiculously excited about the daughter she carried. They hadn't shared the gender news with anyone else, but Willow could hardly wait to make use of the pretty clothes she had begun to collect.

Even as a toddler, Hari was very much a little boy, stomping through mud and puddles and shouting with excitement as he climbed and jumped and toppled. Of course, their daughter might well be a little tomboy, just as energetic, but Willow knew that she would at least be able to enjoy dressing her daughter in pretty clothes until she became more mobile.

'Happy Birthday, *balmaa*,' Jai husked in her ear, breathing in the rich coconut scent of her tumbling strawberry-blond hair as he pressed a kiss to her shoulder and folded her back against his tall, powerful body.

A split second later, he stepped back to slowly slide a necklace round her slender throat, tipping her head forward to clasp it at her nape. Her fingers lifted to touch the sparkling diamond heart and she whirled with a smile in the circle of his arms to stretch up and find his mouth for herself. Excitement buzzed through her, an ache stirring in her pelvis as he crushed her against him, his urgency only matching her own, because Jai had been away on a business trip for a week and she had missed him.

'I was scared you wouldn't make it back in time,' she confided breathlessly against his shoulder.

'I would never miss your birthday,' Jai censured, watching her finger the delicate heart at her throat. 'That's my heart you hold and it *always* brings me home again.'

Willow giggled. 'You're getting almost romantic,' she teased. 'We should go downstairs and see our guests.'

'My mother was holding the fort when I arrived.'

'Milly is a terrific social asset,' Willow agreed, thinking of the mother-in-law she had never expected to have and her warm relationship with her and Jai's stepfather, Steven, a quiet, retiring older man with a delightful sense of humour.

Over the past two years, their family circle had expanded exponentially, but it was a comfortable and caring expansion, which both of them valued. Jai had dealt with his disillusionment over the father he had once idolised and moved on to develop a strong, deep bond with the mother he had been denied in childhood. He had also become acquainted with his maternal grandfather, the current Duke, who was almost ninety years old. Jai did think, though, that it was sad that his mother had never had another child and that he had no siblings, only stepbrothers and a stepsister, whom they only saw at occasional family events.

Even so, his aunt, Jivika, and her husband were regular visitors, along with various other, more distant relatives. Indeed, Jai and Willow had so many invitations out that they had to pick and choose which they could attend and sometimes it was a relief to return to the tranquillity of the Lake Palace, where life was a little less hectic and they could spend more time together as a couple.

Willow had become broody once Hari outgrew the

nursery and turned into a leaping, bounding bundle of energy, no longer content to be cuddled for longer than ten seconds, unless of course he was ill or overtired. She had conceived quickly, and her second pregnancy was proving much easier than the first. She thought that was very probably because she was much less stressed this time and was able to rest whenever she liked.

'You're spoilt rotten!' Shelley had teased her on her last visit to Chandrapur. She was able to see her best friend regularly now because Shelley had more holiday leave in her new job managing a small boutique hotel, which belonged to Jai's cousins. In any case, Willow and Jai spent every spring and summer in London in addition to returning there every year to enjoy a special Christmas at the town house. And when Hari started school, they would be in London even more because Jai did not want his son to board as he had done until he was old enough to make that choice for himself.

And Shelley had spoken the truth, Willow acknowledged with quiet satisfaction, because Jai *did* spoil her and he did make her very, very happy. He also built up her confidence where her father had continually taken her down. Only weeks ago, she had made her first public speech on behalf of the homeless charity she had chosen as closest to her heart from the many supported by the Singh Foundation. Jai's words of praise had made her heart sing and nobody would ever have guessed by his demeanour that he had listened to her rehearse that same speech ten times over.

Now, meeting the arctic-blue intensity of his loving gaze, Willow had everything she'd ever wanted and much that she had not even dared to dream of having, because Jai loved her and their son as much as he loved being part of a family.

'I am crazy about you,' he husked as they descended the stairs to the noisy hubbub of their chattering guests. 'I counted the days until I could come home, and home is always where *you* are, *soniyaa*.'

'I love you too,' she whispered dreamily as his hand engulfed hers, and she whipped round where she stood to claim his sensual mouth for herself again. 'And on *your* birthday promise we'll have a private party for *two*.'

'We're having a very private party for two when everyone's gone home tonight,' Jai assured her, soft and low, running a slow, caressing hand down over her taut spine, making her quiver…

* * * * *

HPCNMRA0220

#3797 DEMANDING HIS BILLION-DOLLAR HEIR
by Pippa Roscoe

Maria was the only woman to see the man behind incredibly wealthy Matthieu's scars. Yet, to protect her, he pushed her away. Now Maria is back, with an announcement that leads the tycoon to question everything: *"I'm pregnant."*

#3798 REVELATIONS OF A SECRET PRINCESS
by Annie West

To find her daughter, stolen from her at birth, Carolina will do *anything*. Including masquerading as a nanny! Jake, her daughter's uncle, is all that's standing in the way. If only her body got the message he's the enemy...

#3799 THE RETURN OF HER BILLIONAIRE HUSBAND
by Melanie Milburne

Juliette is determined to forget her glamorous marriage to billionaire Joe. It began with an intense passion she'd only ever dreamed of, and ended in heartbreak. Now it's time to go their separate ways...or *is* it?

#3800 THE SCANDAL BEHIND THE ITALIAN'S WEDDING
by Millie Adams

Min will do *anything* to protect the baby in her arms, including asking billionaire Dante to make her his bride. And if their scandalous wedding isn't enough, once they get to paradise Min has another revelation...

"Why did you do it, Minerva?"

"I'm sorry. I really didn't do it to cause you trouble. But I'm being
threatened, and so is Isabella, and in order to protect us both I needed to
come up with an alternative paternity story."

"An alternative paternity story?"

She winced. "Yes. Her father is after her."

He eyed her with great skepticism. "I didn't think you knew who her
father was."

She didn't know whether to be shocked, offended or pleased that he
thought her capable of having an anonymous interlude.

For heaven's sake, she'd only ever been kissed one time in her life. A
regrettable evening out with Katie in Rome where she'd tried to enjoy the
pulsing music in the club, but had instead felt overheated and on the verge
of a seizure.

She'd danced with a man in a shiny shirt—and she even knew his name
because she wouldn't even dance with a man without an introduction—and
he'd kissed her on the dance floor. It had been wet and he'd tasted of liquor
and she'd feigned a headache after and taken a cab back to the hostel they'd
been staying in.

The idea of hooking up with someone in a circumstance like that made
her want to peel her own skin off.

"Of course I know who he is. Unfortunately…the full implications of
who he is did not become clear until later."

"What does that mean?"

She could tell him the truth now, but something stopped her. Maybe it
was admitting Isabella wasn't her daughter, which always caught her in the
chest and made her feel small. Like she'd stolen her and like what they had
was potentially fragile, temporary and shaky.

Or maybe it was trust. Dante was a good man. Going off the fact he had rescued her from a fall, and helped her up when her knee was skinned, and bailed her out after her terrible humiliation in high school.

But to trust him with the truth was something she simply wasn't brave enough to do.

Her life, Isabella's life, was at risk, and she'd lied on livestream in front of the world.

Her bravery was tapped out.

"Her father is part of an organized-crime family. Obviously something unknown to me at the time of her…you know. And he's after her. He's after us."

"Are you telling me that you're in actual danger?"

"Yes. And really, the only hope I have is convincing him that he isn't actually the father."

"And you think that will work?"

"It's the only choice I have. I need your protection."

He regarded her with dark, fathomless eyes, and yet again, she felt like he was peering at her as though she were a girl and not a woman at all. A naughty child, in fact. Then something in his expression shifted.

It shamed her a little that this was so like when he'd come to her rescue at the party. That she was manipulating his pity for her. Her own pathetic nature being what called to him yet again.

But she would lay down any and all pride for Isabella, and she'd do it willingly.

"If she were, in fact my child, then we would be family."

"I…I suppose," she said.

"There will need to be photographs of us together, as I would not be a neglectful father."

"No, indeed."

"Of course, you know that if Isabella were really my child there would be only one thing for us to do."

"Do I?"

"Yes." He began to pace, like a caged tiger trying to find a weak spot in his cage. And suddenly he stopped, and she had the terrible feeling that the tiger had found what he'd been looking for. "Yes. Of course there is only one option."

"And that is?"

"You have to marry me."

Don't miss
The Scandal Behind the Italian's Wedding
available March 2020 wherever
Harlequin Presents books and ebooks are sold.

Harlequin.com

HPEXP0220